COPYCAT KILLER

LAURA SCOTT

If you purchased this book without a cover you should be aware that this book is stolen property. It was reported as "unsold and destroyed" to the publisher, and neither the author nor the publisher has received any payment for this "stripped book."

Special thanks and acknowledgment are given to Laura Scott for her contribution to the True Blue K-9 Unit: Brooklyn miniseries.

Recycling programs for this product may not exist in your area.

ISBN-13: 978-1-335-57442-8

Copycat Killer

Copyright © 2020 by Harlequin Books S.A.

All rights reserved. No part of this book may be used or reproduced in any manner whatsoever without written permission except in the case of brief quotations embodied in critical articles and reviews.

This is a work of fiction. Names, characters, places and incidents are either the product of the author's imagination or are used fictitiously. Any resemblance to actual persons, living or dead, businesses, companies, events or locales is entirely coincidental.

This edition published by arrangement with Harlequin Books S.A.

For questions and comments about the quality of this book, please contact us at CustomerService@Harlequin.com.

Love Inspired
22 Adelaide St. West, 40th Floor
Toronto, Ontario M5H 4E3, Canada
www.Harlequin.com

Printed in U.S.A.

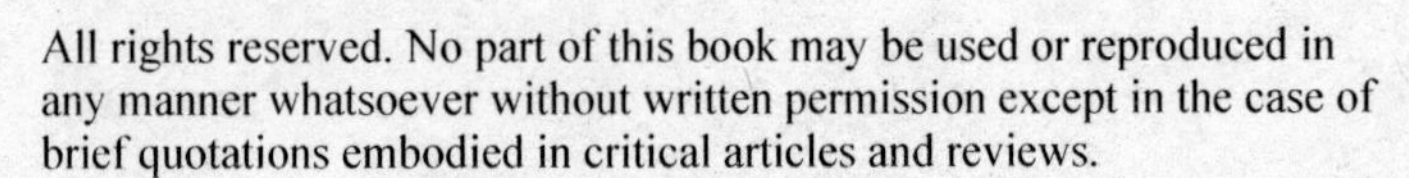

Nate heard Willow scream.

He wheeled around the corner, his heart lodged in his throat.

Lucy was crying, loud screeching sobs. "Aunt Willow! Aunt Willow! Come back!"

Someone dressed in black with a hat pulled low over his forehead was dragging Willow toward a sedan.

"Stop! Police!" Nate shouted. Realizing he might be too late, he reached down and released his yellow Lab's leash. "Get him, Murphy. Get him!"

His K-9 partner took off running. The man's eyes widened and he pushed Willow to the ground and raced away, the dog giving chase.

TRUE BLUE K-9 UNIT: BROOKLYN

These police officers fight for justice
with the help of their brave canine partners.

Copycat Killer by Laura Scott, April 2020
Chasing Secrets by Heather Woodhaven, May 2020
Deadly Connection by Lenora Worth, June 2020
Explosive Situation by Terri Reed, July 2020
Tracking a Kidnapper by Valerie Hansen, August 2020
Scene of the Crime by Sharon Dunn, September 2020
Cold Case Pursuit by Dana Mentink, October 2020
Delayed Justice by Shirlee McCoy, November 2020
True Blue K-9 Unit Christmas: Brooklyn by Laura Scott
and Maggie K. Black, December 2020

Archbold Community Library
205 Stryker Street
Archbold, OH 43502

Laura Scott is a nurse by day and an author by night. She has always loved romance and read faith-based books by Grace Livingston Hill in her teenage years. She's thrilled to have published over twenty-five books for Love Inspired Suspense. She has two adult children and lives in Milwaukee, Wisconsin, with her husband of over thirty years. Please visit Laura at laurascottbooks.com.

Books by Laura Scott

Love Inspired Suspense

True Blue K-9 Unit: Brooklyn

Copycat Killer

Justice Seekers

Soldier's Christmas Secrets

Callahan Confidential

Shielding His Christmas Witness
The Only Witness
Christmas Amnesia
Shattered Lullaby
Primary Suspect
Protecting His Secret Son

True Blue K-9 Unit

Blind Trust
True Blue K-9 Unit Christmas
"Holiday Emergency"

Visit the Author Profile page at Harlequin.com for more titles.

Blessed is he whose transgression is forgiven,
whose sin is covered.
—*Psalms* 32:1

This book is dedicated to Lisa Collins, who loves dogs as much as I do. I'm so happy to have our families forever joined by the marriage of our children.

ONE

Willow Emery approached her brother and sister-in-law's two-story home in Brooklyn, New York, with a deep sense of foreboding. The white paint on the front door of the yellow brick building was cracked and peeling, the windows covered with grime. A short decorative black iron fence surrounded the small front yard, revealing empty food wrappers and cigarette butts strewn across the tiny lawn. She swallowed hard, hating that her three-year-old niece, Lucy, lived in such deplorable conditions.

Steeling her resolve, she straightened her shoulders. This time, she wouldn't be dissuaded so easily. Her older brother, Alex, and his wife, Debra, had to agree that Lucy deserved better.

Squeak. Squeak. The rusty gate moving in

the breeze caused a chill to ripple through her. Why was it open? She hurried forward and her stomach knotted when she found the front door hanging ajar. The tiny hairs on the back of her neck lifted in alarm and a shiver rippled down her spine.

Something was wrong. Very wrong.

Thunk. The loud sound startled her. Was that a door closing? Or something worse? Her heart pounded in her chest and her mouth went dry. Following her gut instincts, Willow quickly pushed the front door open and crossed the threshold. The assault of sour milk mixed with awful bodily odors hit hard. Bile rose in her throat as she strained to listen. “Alex? Lucy?”

There was no answer, only the echo of soft, hiccuping sobs.

“Lucy!” Hurrying now, she followed the sound through the kitchen, briefly taking note of the dozens of empty liquor bottles and overflowing dirty dishes in the sink. Reaching the living room, she stumbled to an abrupt halt, her feet seemingly glued to the floor. Lucy was kneeling near her mother, crying. Alex and Debra were lying facedown, unmoving and not breathing, blood seeping out from beneath them.

Were those bullet holes between their shoulder blades? Her brother's head was turned to the side, his eyes vacant and staring. *No! Alex!* A wave of nausea had her placing a hand over her stomach.

She locked her gaze on her niece. "Lucy?"

The girl lifted her head. Her tearstained face tugged at her heart. "Aunt Willow, Mommy and Daddy won't wake up," she sobbed.

"Lucy, sweetie, it's okay. Come with me, baby." Hands shaking, Willow stepped carefully, avoiding the large pool of blood, until she was close enough to lift Lucy up and into her arms.

Lucy didn't stop crying, but curled her arms around her neck, clinging tightly. Willow pressed a hand to her niece's wavy blond hair, holding her close for a long moment. Then she shifted the girl to her hip, bent down and pressed her fingers against her brother's neck, searching for a pulse.

Nothing.

A sob rose in her throat, but she fought it back. With trembling fingers, she checked Debra, too. Still nothing. Should she try CPR?

Remembering the thud gave her pause. She glanced furtively over her shoulder toward the single bedroom on the main floor. The door was closed. What if the gunman was still here? Waiting? Hiding?

The terrifying possibility had her spinning away and retracing her steps through the disgusting kitchen and out the front door. She stumbled through the lawn, kicking something that crinkled beneath her foot out of the way, until she reached the sidewalk.

Fumbling for her phone with her right hand, she tried to understand what had just happened. Who had shot Alex and Debra? And why? What caused the thudding noise?

What had her older brother gotten himself into?

She pulled herself together, knowing she needed to call the police, to get help.

She dialed 911 and pressed the phone to her ear, one arm still securely wrapped around Lucy.

"This is the operator. What's the nature of your emergency?"

"My brother and his wife have been shot. Please send the police right away!"

"Are you safe, ma'am?"

Good question. The back of her neck tingled with fear and she whipped around, frantically searching for something, anything, out of place. She wished for a place to hide. There was a small tree nearby, and she instinctively made her way toward it, cowering beneath the branches that were just now budding leaves, pressing her back against the slim trunk. "I—I don't know."

"What's the address?"

She rattled off the number of the house on Thirty-Fifth Street. "It's off Linden Boulevard in East Flatbush. Please hurry!"

"I'm calling the closest officer to your location. Please stay on the line."

"Just get here, soon!" Willow didn't want to stay on the line; she needed both of her arms to hold Lucy. Leaving the phone on speaker, she tucked it into the back pocket of her jeans. She held her niece, stroking a soothing hand down Lucy's back, murmuring reassuringly in her ear. Vehicles moved up and down Linden Boulevard, yet Willow still felt vulnerable. Exposed. What if they were still in danger?

What if the gunman was out there, watching her?

She swept her gaze over the area again, but still didn't see anything suspicious. Yet she couldn't shake the itchy feeling of being watched. The narrow tree offered little protection. Where should she go? What should she do? She momentarily closed her eyes, fighting panic.

Dear Lord, keep us safe in Your care!

The whispered prayer helped to calm her irrational need to run far, far away. Her apartment was in Bay Ridge, too far to walk, let alone run. Not to mention the bloodstains on Lucy's clothes would draw attention to them. Willow took several deep breaths, knowing she needed to relax so Lucy wouldn't pick up on her fear.

"It's okay, Lucy. We're fine. We're going to be just fine."

Lucy's crying slowly quieted, but the little girl didn't release her deathlike grip, as if afraid of being left behind.

A white SUV with the blue NYPD K-9 logo along the side and a red flashing light on its dashboard came barreling down the street toward them, abruptly pulling over to the curb. A tall, lean blond officer dressed in a black uniform came out from behind the wheel, weapon held ready. Moving quickly, he opened his hatch, letting a beautiful yellow Lab wearing a K9 vest out of the back.

"Stay where you are," the officer said when she moved from the relative safety of the tree to head toward him. His gaze raked the area as he hurried over. His name tag identified his last name as Detective Slater. "What happened? Are you both okay?"

"Yes. But I found my brother and his wife d—" She glanced at Lucy and amended what she'd been about to say. "Um, hurt.

Both the gate and the front door were hanging ajar when I arrived." She shivered, the reality of it all just starting to sink in. "The bedroom door was closed. I'm afraid someone is still inside."

He nodded but didn't move away. He spoke into his radio, asking for an ETA of his backup. She couldn't deny the overwhelming relief she and Lucy were no longer alone.

"I need you to both wait inside my SUV." He took her elbow and urged her toward the police vehicle just as his backup arrived. "Stay inside. I'll be back soon."

She didn't argue, feeling much safer inside the car. She continued to hold Lucy on her lap as she watched Detective Slater and two uniformed cops go inside the house with their weapons up in a two-handed grip.

The seconds went by with excruciating slowness and she buried her face against Lucy's hair, still grappling with what had happened.

A sharp rap against the window startled her. She relaxed when she saw Detective

Slater standing there. He opened the door and she slid out, standing to face him. She had to look up at him, which was unusual as she was taller than most women. His expression was kind, but grim. “I’m sorry for your loss. The house is clear. There’s no one inside.”

Sorry for your loss. She momentarily closed her eyes and rested her cheek on Lucy’s head. She’d known her brother and his wife were dead.

Murdered.

Why? She couldn’t imagine anyone wanting to kill her brother and his wife. And what about Lucy?

Was the little girl in danger, too?

Nate Slater kept his gaze on the tall, pretty woman holding the cute little girl, fearing she might collapse under the weight of the bad news.

He tucked a hand beneath her elbow to hold her steady. “Are you sure you’re okay?”

She shook her head, but then nodded. Shrugged. “I have to be.”

He understood where she was coming

from. The poor woman and the little girl had witnessed the result of violence that most only read about. Going through an ordeal like this couldn't be easy for either of them.

As part of the newly established Brooklyn K-9 Unit, an offshoot of the original NYC K-9 Command Unit that was still located in Queens, he and his four-legged partner, Murphy, had been dealing with another issue close by when he'd gotten the call to come to this location. The Brooklyn K-9 Unit responded to calls across all five boroughs of New York City, the canine partners' specializations aiding the officers in investigating crimes and tracking down perpetrators. Nate's dog was cross-trained in a variety of skills. "I need to ask a few questions, Ms…."

"Willow. Willow Emery. This is my niece, Lucy Emery." She raised her chin and the stubborn flash in her light brown eyes was surprisingly reassuring. "I'll tell you whatever you need to know."

"You mentioned the front door wasn't

closed all the way. Did your brother normally keep the place locked up?"

"Yes. Always. That's why the noise was so jarring."

"Noise?" His interest was piqued.

She nodded. "A thud, like a door banging closed."

"Or the sound of gunfire?"

Her eyes rounded in horror. "No!"

The timing seemed off, but he continued. "Okay, and normally the back door would also be locked?" He'd noticed the back door had been closed, but not locked. It appeared the intruder may have been let in from the front, maybe someone the victims had known. Something must have gone wrong, and they'd been shot in the back, the killer escaping out the back door.

"I think so, yes. Unless they were outside. The back patio has a little fence around it, similar to the one in the front."

Yeah, he'd noticed the fence, more for decoration than anything else, and not very high, so any able-bodied person could easily climb over.

He felt certain the perp had escaped that way and itched to begin searching. But he needed more information, something to go on.

"Lucy?" He waited for the little girl to look up at him. "Did you see anything?"

She didn't answer, and Willow lightly stroked her hair.

"It's okay, tell the policeman what you saw."

"Bad clown."

Lucy's whisper gave him pause. Nate leaned closer, trying to appear nonthreatening. "What did you say?"

Lucy immediately ducked her head, hiding her face against Willow's neck.

He caught Willow's gaze, silently pleading. He needed to question the little girl further.

"Lucy, you're safe here with me and Detective Slater. But we really need to know, did you see someone hurt your mommy and daddy?" Willow's tone was soft, gentle.

There was a momentary hesitation, then the little girl gave a tentative nod.

Nate's pulse spiked with adrenaline. A possible witness, albeit a very young one.

But maybe old enough to provide something for them to go on. "Can you tell me what you saw?"

Lucy hunched her shoulders without responding. Long seconds ticked by before the child finally said, "The bad clown weared black."

Bad clown wearing black? Nate still didn't quite get it, but now they had a description to go on. The two uniformed officers who'd helped him clear the house crossed over to join him, as another K-9 officer from his unit, Vivienne Armstrong, and her black-and-white border collie partner, Hank, arrived. Hank's specialty was search and rescue, and Nate was glad to have the excellent tracker on the hunt.

"Nate? What's going on?" Vivienne asked.

He stepped back from Willow and Lucy, instinctively taking charge of the scene. "Two DOAs inside, house has been cleared but it's possible the perp went out the back. I need one NYPD officer to stay here with Willow and Lucy. The rest of us need to fan out and search for the killer, likely dressed in black and possibly wearing a mask." He couldn't be certain what Lucy meant by clown and thought the perp could be wearing something plastic over his or her face.

"I'll stay," Officer Klein volunteered.

"Good. Murphy and I will go south. Vivienne, you and Hank head east. I need you, Officer Talbot, to head west," he directed. He didn't think anyone would have come north toward the front of the house. "Keep your radio frequency open and if you find someone suspicious, proceed with caution. Perp is likely armed with a gun."

"Got it," Vivienne said as the rest nodded in agreement.

The three of them split up, he and Murphy taking the path he thought was more likely the one the killer used as an escape route. The Holy Saints Cemetery was located a few blocks to the south of the Emery property, and he thought there was a good chance the "bad clown wearing black" had gone that way.

A quick glance at the crime scene hadn't revealed anything left behind by the perp.

He wanted to stay to search more closely but couldn't deny a keen sense of urgency. How much time had passed since the emergency call Willow had made? Five minutes? Seven?

Too long.

He and Murphy reached the twin dark gray stone arches of the cemetery entrance in less than two minutes. Entering the cemetery grounds, he examined the soft earth around the tombstones searching for signs of footprints. After the April rainstorm late yesterday afternoon, which had softened the ground and eliminated most of the leftover remnants of winter snow, he was hopeful no one could cut through without leaving evidence behind.

A partial footprint in the mud caught his gaze. It was wide on top and deep, making him think it was made by a man, maybe even someone running. Expanding his search, he tried to find another one that looked similar, in an effort to provide a direction the perp may have taken. He wanted to use the footprint as a scent source for

Murphy to follow, but knew that without a second footprint indicating evidence of running away, he couldn't be sure it was left by the killer. He didn't want Murphy to search for the wrong person.

He searched for another fifteen minutes but came up empty.

Either the guy had stayed to the paved walkway snaking around the grounds or he hadn't come this way at all.

Nate didn't want to give up, but after more fruitless searching, he cued his radio. "Any sign of the perp?"

A chorus of negatives echoed from the other officers.

"Let's call it off." He didn't want to but didn't see the point of continuing a random search. In his gut he felt the killer was long gone, but he'd hoped for something, anything, to go on. "Thanks for your help."

Several ten-fours echoed from the radio.

Nate and Murphy double-timed it back to the scene of the murders. He slowed to a walk when he came around the Emery house.

Willow was sitting crossways on the passenger seat of his SUV with the door open, still holding Lucy on her lap. He noticed she was wearing soft blue jeans and a thin pink hoodie in deference to the sixty-degree spring day. There were many vehicles parked on the street, so he wasn't sure if she'd driven over or if she'd arrived via subway or bus. The little girl was wearing a cheerful yellow top with a flared hem over yellow bloodstained leggings. Officer Klein, the uniform who'd stayed behind, remained standing nearby.

"Doggy," Lucy said, pointing at Murphy. "Big doggy."

He crossed over to where Willow and Lucy were, dropping to his knees so he was eye level with both Murphy and the little girl. He wondered why the child had been spared. Because she was in another room? Or because the perp drew some invisible line at shooting an innocent child?

"This is Murphy." He introduced the K-9 again. "Friend, Murphy." He touched both Willow and Lucy, while repeating, "Friend."

"Hold out your hand for the doggy to sniff," Willow encouraged.

Lucy held out her hand, smiling a bit when Murphy's nose touched her skin. "Nice doggy."

"Yes, Murphy is a nice dog. He won't hurt you."

Willow searched his gaze. "Find anything?"

He shook his head. "I'd like to ask Lucy a few more questions if that's okay."

Willow's light brown eyes looked concerned, but she nodded. "Can't hurt to try."

Nate waited until Lucy looked at him, with eyes that were mirror images of Willow's. If he didn't know any better, he'd think they were mother and daughter instead of aunt and niece. "Lucy, can you tell me more about the bad clown that wore black?"

Her tiny brow puckered with fear. "Scary," she whispered.

"I know it was scary," he agreed with a gentle smile. "But you're a brave girl, aren't you? I need you to tell me what the bad clown looked like."

"Big. Mean." Lucy scrunched up her face. "Clown face with blue hair on top." She lifted a hand to her own hair as if to describe what she meant.

Blue hair? His chest tightened at her description. Twenty years ago—today—there had been a double murder in Brooklyn. Two of his colleagues, a brother and a sister, Bradley and Penelope McGregor, then just kids, had lost their parents. Bradley, fourteen, had been at a friend's house, and four-year-old Penelope, left unharmed like Lucy, had been the only witness. She'd described the killer as a clown—with blue hair. He'd been thinking about the cold case today, as he knew the entire unit was, because of the anniversary. Twenty years unsolved. "You're sure the hair was blue?"

She bobbed her head. "Blue like my dolly."

Her dolly? He lifted a brow and glanced up at Willow, who nodded.

"Yes, she has a doll with bright blue hair."

"Okay, blue hair on the top of the clown face," he repeated. "Did you notice anything else about him?"

She shook her head. "Too scary."

He imagined she'd hid her face and hoped that she hadn't seen her parents being murdered in cold blood. He thought again how odd it was they'd both been shot in the back. As if they'd been heading out of the kitchen, toward the living room. Is that where Lucy had been? Or were they going there for some other reason?

No way to know for sure. The place was a mess, but it was difficult to tell if it had been searched by the killer. After making a mental note to tell the crime scene techs to make the living room a priority when looking for evidence, he turned his attention to the little girl. "What else, Lucy? Were you in the house when he came inside?"

Lucy shook her head, reaching out to pet Murphy's sleek fur.

"No? Where were you?" Willow asked.

"Outside playing." Lucy looked over toward the front of the house. "Mommy and Daddy were inside."

Nate's gaze sharpened. "He came up the sidewalk and into the fenced-in front yard?"

"Yes. He gived me a toy and told me to stay outside." Her lower lip trembled, and Nate was concerned she might cry.

"It's okay, Lucy, you're safe with us," Willow said, gently hugging her. "What kind of toy?"

"A monkey." Lucy's face crumpled. "I don't want it anymore."

A monkey? He sucked in a breath. The McGregors' killer had also given Penelope a stuffed monkey. What was going on here?

"Are you sure?" he asked hoarsely. "Was it a stuffed monkey?"

Lucy bobbed her head up and down. "I left it outside when I heard the loud noise, but I don't want it anymore. I want my mommy!"

"Shh, it's okay. I'm here, Lucy." Willow cuddled her close.

Nate rocked back on his heels, stunned speechless. The clown face with blue hair on top, two bullet holes in Lucy's parents and a stuffed monkey.

The exact same MO as the twenty-year-old unsolved McGregor murders. The brutal slaying of the parents of fellow Brooklyn

K-9 detective Bradley McGregor and his sister, desk clerk Penelope McGregor.

Down to the very last detail.

The idea that a killer from twenty years ago was still out there concerned him.

They needed to get this guy, and soon. Before anyone else ended up hurt, or worse, dead.

TWO

At first Willow thought Lucy was imagining things. Mean clown with blue hair? Wearing black? Giving her a stuffed monkey and telling her to stay outside? But she vaguely remembered her foot hitting something soft yet crinkly as she crossed the front lawn, and the shock that rippled over Nate Slater's face was all too real. "What's wrong? Do you know who did this?"

Nate shook his head, averting his gaze. "No, but we're going to do our best to find the person responsible." He turned and smiled gently at Lucy. "You're very brave, Lucy. Thank you for telling me what you saw." He stood. "Come, Murphy. Vivienne? Will you and Hank give me a moment?"

"Sure." The pretty, dark-haired, dark-eyed K-9 cop hurried over and followed as Nate and Murphy headed purposefully to the front of the house, no doubt searching for the stuffed monkey.

Lucy burrowed against Willow. She cuddled the little girl close, knowing her niece was traumatized, and silently promised to make sure Lucy was set up with a child psychologist as soon as possible.

She also hoped the little girl wasn't in any sort of ongoing danger. Granted, the mean clown had tried to hide his identity, but she couldn't afford to ignore the possibility that he might return to finish what he'd started.

Nate returned, a small stuffed animal enclosed in what appeared to be two evidence bags. "Lucy, is this the monkey? Did the bad clown give it to you in a bag?"

Lucy lifted her head from Willow's shoulder and nodded.

He glanced at Vivienne. "This guy is smart, knew enough to minimize the scent by wearing gloves and putting the toy in a bag. Murphy wasn't able to pick up the scent to track. We can hope to lift prints from the plastic bag surrounding the monkey, but I'm not holding my breath."

Vivienne grimaced. "Nate, you'd better call Sarge, give him the update."

"Yeah." He dropped his tone making it difficult to hear. "Gavin Sutherland is going to take this personally. You know how much he feels responsible for Bradley and Penny McGregor, especially today. It's not going to be easy to tell them their parents' killer may be back." Nate tucked the double-bagged monkey in his pocket and reached for his phone.

Her gaze clung to Nate Slater's tall, muscular figure as he contacted his boss. She couldn't help overhearing pieces of his conversation.

"Gavin? Slater here. Listen, this is big. I've got two dead victims, parents of a child who survived, and the perp's MO is exactly like the McGregor case from twenty years ago down to the last detail, including the stuffed monkey."

Nate fell silent as he listened to his boss.

"I agree, the murderer must have resurfaced again, but why? Where's he been all this time—"

"Is there anything I can get you?" Vivienne interrupted with a polite smile.

Willow flushed, wondering if the female K-9 officer knew she'd been eavesdropping.

"Yes, I—uh, would like to get some of Lucy's things, like her clothes and a few favorite toys."

Vivienne frowned. "I'm sorry, but I don't think you can take anything out until the crime scene has been processed." The officer's gaze sharpened at something over her head. "It appears the ME and crime scene techs are here now."

Willow turned in time to see two large vehicles. The dark van must belong to the coroner; the other was a white box truck with the NYPD logo that parked directly in front of Detective Slater's SUV. She watched as a petite blonde with dimples emerged from behind the wheel, crossing over to join them.

"Darcy, this is Willow and Lucy Emery," Vivienne said by way of introduction.

"Darcy Fields is a forensic specialist with NYPD who often responds to our cases."

Willow nodded a greeting, the names already becoming a jumble in her mind.

Except for Nate Slater. And Murphy.

Nate disconnected from the call and crossed over to rejoin them. "Darcy, after you process the main crime scene, I want you to do a thorough sweep of the living room to see if you can find anything that may be hidden."

"Hidden in the living room?" Willow asked. "What makes you think that?"

The three of them glanced at her as if they'd forgotten she was there.

"No special reason," Nate hedged. "Just a hunch."

"Got it," Darcy agreed. The bright paisley scarf around her throat was a burst of scarlet against the tan khaki slacks and white blouse. She hurried back to the van and began donning protective gear.

Hunch? About something hidden? Willow realized Nate and Vivienne weren't going to clue her in as to what their investigation was revealing; it must be against some sort of cop rules. She frowned, thinking over her brief foray into the house. The kitchen had been a disaster, but she'd seen it that way before. The living room had been unusually messy, as well. Two months ago, the last time she'd confronted her brother and his wife about Lucy's welfare, it had looked much the same.

It hurt to remember how she'd found Lucy hungry and wearing dirty clothes, with little food appropriate for a young child in the house. Alex had quickly sent Debra out to pick up some groceries, then told Willow to mind her own business.

She'd been tempted to report Alex and Debra to Child Protective Services, but decided to give them a chance to do better. To make things right. But as the weeks passed without a response to her many phone calls to Alex, she'd come to face off with them in person. To tell them to voluntarily give her temporary custody of Lucy or she'd notify CPS.

Now they were dead. *Dead!* It all seemed

so surreal. As if this nightmare was happening to someone else, not to her.

Which brought her back to the present. Why was Nate focused on something being hidden in the living room? It didn't make sense.

As Lucy turned in her lap, reaching out to pet Murphy again, it hit her.

Alex and Debra had been shot in the back, lying facedown just inside the living room. She could almost imagine the shooter being in the kitchen, firing as they were walking, or maybe even running, toward the living room.

Her stomach churned. Had they been trying to get to something they'd hidden for safekeeping? She was thankful that Lucy had been outside when the "bad clown" had killed her parents. But that didn't prevent her from wishing she had called CPS months ago.

If she had, maybe her brother and his wife would have pulled themselves together, doing the right thing to get Lucy back. Had they been involved in something shady that had gotten them killed? Or was it a random murder?

Anyway, now it was too late. They were gone. And she couldn't turn back the clock.

"Aunt Willow, I'm hungry." Lucy's plaintive tone made her realize how long they'd been outside.

"Okay, hang on, I have some animal crackers with me." She dug in her oversize shoulder bag, finding the animal-shaped vanilla crackers. She'd purposely brought them along in case there wasn't any food in the house like last time.

Lucy nibbled on a cracker, her attitude subdued rather than her usual playful self. Willow's heart ached for the little girl.

"Excuse me." Willow lifted her hand to get Nate's or Vivienne's attention. "How much longer do we need to stay? Am I able to take Lucy home with me?"

Nate and Vivienne exchanged a long glance before Nate nodded. "We need to contact Child Protective Services first to let them know the situation. Where do you live?"

"Bay Ridge."

His brow levered upward. “That’s where our K-9 headquarters is located.” He glanced at his watch. “Give us a few more minutes. Vivienne, will you get an okay from Child Protective Services on Willow taking Lucy home tonight? Once they approve, I’ll drive Willow and Lucy there.”

“Sure.” Vivienne moved away to use her phone.

“Okay.” Frankly, she wouldn’t mind a ride; the idea of carrying Lucy through the subway wasn’t appealing. She gazed wistfully at her brother’s place. If only she could pick out a few things, like Lucy’s stroller, her clothes and toys, it would be an easier transition for the little girl.

Lucy rested against her, eating another animal cracker. She pressed a kiss to the top of Lucy’s wavy blond hair, reveling in the calming scent of baby shampoo.

Lucy was safe, and that was all that mattered. She had some money saved up. She could buy whatever Lucy needed.

Willow would do everything in her power

to keep Lucy in a safe, warm, stable and loving home.

From this moment forward and for the rest of their lives.

Nate's phone vibrated with an incoming text message. He tore his gaze from Willow and Lucy, pulled the device from his pocket, and read Penelope McGregor's note.

Today is the 20th anniversary of my parents' murders. The same MO can't be a coincidence.

Nate shot a quick message back in return. Don't worry, we'll figure it out.

Still reeling from the similarities between the recent Emery double murder and the twenty-year-old McGregor cold case murder of Penny and Bradley's parents, he mentally reviewed the scene of the crime.

April 14, the exact same date with the same MO, all the way down to the clown face with blue hair and the cheap stuffed monkey. He shivered just thinking about the cold case. Forty-year-old Eddie and

Anna McGregor had been killed in their Brooklyn home, each shot at close range. Their son, Bradley, just fourteen, had been at a sleepover at a friend's house. Daughter Penny, just four years old, had witnessed the murders. To make the case even more heartbreaking, Bradley had been considered a suspect for a long time. His parents had been neglectful, same as the Emerys, and Bradley had been known to fiercely argue with them, particularly as it concerned his little sister. There had been no evidence connecting Bradley to the murders, so he'd been dropped from the suspect list, but the taint had never quite left him. Bradley and Penny had been taken in by the lead detective on the case and his wife, and the dedicated cop had gone to his grave not knowing who'd killed the McGregors.

Nate knew that Bradley—and Penny—wanted to rectify that. Now, suddenly, there was movement on the case, a break. Because another set of parents had died with the remarkably same MO.

The murderer was back after twenty years. Why? And where had he been all this time?

"What did Gavin have to say?" Vivienne asked, interrupting his thoughts.

Gavin had been rattled by the report of the same MO; Nate had heard it in his voice, even if the sarge worked hard to hide it. "He's worried about how Bradley and Penny are handling the news. Once the media gets wind of it..." He shook his head.

"It won't be pretty," Vivienne agreed. She glanced around the crime scene, where a dozen cops and techs were busy processing the evidence. The two EMTs had finally left, with only the coroner's van and the white crime scene box truck remaining on scene. "CPS agreed to let Willow take temporary custody of Lucy. I'm heading out, unless you need something?"

He was about to say no, but then hesitated. There was one difference between the twenty-year-old case and this current one.

Half of a leather watch band had been found at the scene of the McGregor murders. The DNA had been tested from dead skin cells lifted from the inside of the band, but so far no match in the national crime DNA data bank had been found.

He wondered if there was anything left behind by the murderer in the Emery case, other than the stuffed monkey encased in plastic. He thought about the fenced-in backyard. He'd been so focused on finding the gunman and then the monkey that he hadn't searched closely for clues.

"Stay here next to Willow and Lucy for a few minutes, would you?" He shortened up Murphy's leash. "Come, Murphy."

"Where are you going?" Willow's terse question caught him off guard.

"I'll be back shortly." He flashed a reassuring grin. "I'll take you and Lucy home after I check something out."

Her smile was sad. "Okay."

He understood she wanted to get Lucy out of here, so he quickened his pace. When he'd rounded the backyard earlier in an effort to follow the path the perp may have taken, he hadn't bothered searching for clues. The crime scene techs would be very thorough, but he still wanted to go back to check the ground beyond the house for himself.

Retracing his steps, he closely examined the ground on the other side of the fence, searching for evidence. Footprints, or something the perp may have dropped.

Unfortunately, the backyard butted right up against the road, no soft ground to reveal a footprint similar to what he'd found in the cemetery. He broadened his search outside the property, but still came up empty-handed.

Unless the techs found some kind of DNA evidence inside, they'd have nothing to use as a match for what had been identified on the leather watch band.

Disappointed, he turned back to the Emery crime scene. "Murphy, heel."

The yellow Lab obediently sat at his left side.

"Good boy." He bent over to scratch Murphy behind the ears, then hurried back to where Willow and Lucy waited next to Vivienne.

"I was just explaining to Willow that

a caseworker by the name of Jayne Hendricks will be following up either tomorrow or Tuesday." Vivienne smiled gently. "I'm sure everything will be fine."

Willow nodded. "Okay."

"Ready to go?" he asked.

"Yes, thank you." Willow glanced down at Lucy. "Except I just realized we'll need a child safety seat for your vehicle."

He frowned, understanding her concern. "I'll run and grab one. Vivienne, will you and Hank keep watch?"

"Sure."

As he ran the errand, he thought about Willow and Lucy. There was something vulnerable yet strong about them. As if it was the two of them against the world.

It reminded him of how close he and his mother once were. When he was younger, it had been the two of them against the world, too.

When he returned, he opened the box and pulled out the car seat. Willow took it from him and expertly placed it in the back seat of his SUV.

Nate looked at the petite little girl, noticing again that her yellow outfit carried several dark smears of blood. He'd need to take her clothing in as evidence, which meant she'd need replacements.

"Why don't we stop and pick up a few more things along the way?" he offered. With the traffic, the drive between East Flatbush and Bay Ridge would take a good forty-five minutes. "There's a department store not too far from here."

"Thank you. That would be great."

He wasn't sure why he'd offered to take her home; he wasn't exactly the family kind of guy. Yet it was on the way to the K-9 Unit headquarters, so he told himself it was the decent thing to do.

Willow gently set Lucy in the car seat, while he put Murphy in the back K-9 crate area. Using the rearview mirror, he kept an eye on Lucy as he navigated the traffic toward Bay Ridge.

"Detective Slater?"

He glanced at Willow. "Sounds so formal. Why don't you call me Nate?"

"Um, okay, Nate." She cleared her throat. "I know you can't give me details about the investigation, but I'd like to be kept informed of your progress. I—need to know the person who killed my brother will be punished. No matter what my brother did—" She stopped and swallowed hard before continuing. "He and Debra didn't deserve to be murdered in their home."

"I can't make any promises," he cautioned. "But I'll do my best to keep you updated on the case." Considering the similarities between the Emery murders and the twenty-year-old McGregor case, he felt certain Gavin would fight hard to keep the newly established Brooklyn K-9 Unit on the case. He'd been the first officer on the scene and wanted, needed, to see it through to the end.

"Thank you." Willow ran her fingers through her long straight brown hair. "I still can't believe this happened."

"Was your brother expecting your visit?" He glanced at Willow.

She winced and shook her head. "No, unfortunately he was ignoring my calls. Debra, too. This was my first day off in two weeks, so I decided to confront them face-to-face."

"About what?"

She hesitated, then waved a hand. "You saw the place. Empty liquor bottles, dirty dishes piled up to the cabinets and hardly any decent food. Is that a good environment for a child? I knew Lucy wasn't exactly a planned addition to their family, but I thought they'd settle down, do the right thing." She let out a heavy sigh. "They didn't."

He nodded thoughtfully. Her brother's lifestyle may have made it easier for a stranger to get into their house. Maybe someone who'd confronted them, then fired his weapon as they ran away. But why? That was the nagging question.

If the killer was the same murderer from twenty years ago, he couldn't figure out why they'd struck again, all these years later.

"Oh, there's the store." Willow gestured toward her side of the road.

He'd almost forgotten his promise. He quickly maneuvered over to the right lane, then pulled into the parking lot. The moment he stopped the car, Willow pushed out of her passenger seat and opened the back door to get Lucy from the car seat.

He fetched Murphy, unwilling to leave him in the car, and easily caught up to her. It felt strange to walk into the store with Willow and Lucy. He'd never dated a single mother, or any woman who wanted to settle down. He was keenly aware of the smiles aimed in their direction, as if they were a happy little family.

Maybe because his blond hair was similar to Lucy's, not to mention, Lucy had Willow's cinnamon-brown eyes.

He found himself putting distance between them, instinctively shying away from being associated with the role of husband and father. That was a path he'd never take.

Not with his history.

Willow lifted Lucy into the seat of a shopping cart, then whizzed through the aisles, picking out clothes, a stroller and toys. Then she added groceries before heading over to the checkout lane.

"I'm sure you'll be able to get some things from the house once the scene has been processed," he reminded her.

"I know, but these are essentials." The total was staggering, but she didn't blink as she paid the bill.

He stored most of the items in the back seat while Willow lifted Lucy up and buckled her in.

"Ready?" He glanced at Willow.

For the first time since he'd met her, she offered a genuine smile. The way her entire face brightened made his mouth go dry. Willow was incredibly beautiful, tall and slender like a model might be. "Yes, thank you."

Inwardly shaking his head at his foolishness, he started the SUV. Pulling back into traffic, he decided not to mention that he'd need Lucy's bloodstained clothes as evidence until after they'd reached her apartment. "What's your address?"

She rattled it off and he recognized it as a prewar redbrick apartment building, not far from where their headquarters was located.

"Nice," he said. "A two-bedroom place?"

"No, just one." She glanced back at Lucy and shrugged. "It will have to do for now."

He was curious as to what her job was that allowed her to afford even a one-bedroom in the nice neighborhood, but told himself it wasn't his business. His own single-bedroom apartment had been his mother's, one that he'd inherited after she died. Conveniently located on the ground floor, there was a small yard for Murphy.

Thinking about his mother, and how far they'd come after leaving his abusive father, wasn't helpful. He needed to stay focused on the case at hand, not the disturbing memories of his past.

When he reached her apartment building, she looked at him with uncertainty in her gaze. "Thanks. The killer hid his identity. There's no reason for him to come after us, right? After all, Lucy can't identify him, and I never saw him at all."

He threw the gearshift in Park. "Yes, I wouldn't leave you otherwise. But I'll arrange for a squad car to drive by hourly, just to be extra cautious. Come on, I'll carry your things up for you."

She gave a nod, then slid out of the seat. She set Lucy on her feet, then grabbed the bag of new clothes with one hand and clung to Lucy's tiny fingers with the other. He let Murphy out of the back, then hauled everything else as he followed her and Lucy inside. There was no key to get into the lobby, making him frown. But the lobby was nice, newly renovated with black-and-white tile floors.

"I'm on the seventh floor." She pushed the elevator button and stepped back.

Lucy looked around with wide, curious eyes. Then she lightly stroked Murphy. "Can the doggy stay wif us?"

"No, sweetie, he lives with Detective Nate."

It was on the tip of his tongue to offer to bring Murphy for a visit, but he caught himself in the nick of time.

When the elevator opened, Willow led the way to her apartment, number 706. She had her key but didn't use it. She came to an abrupt stop, then gingerly pushed the door open. He heard her gasp. “Oh no!”

“What is it?” He peered over her shoulder and instantly saw what was wrong.

Willow’s apartment had been thoroughly and completely ransacked.

THREE

Her mouth went desert dry and her heart thudded painfully in her chest. She stared at the horrific invasion of her privacy.

Never in her entire life had she felt so violated.

"Stay back—let me check it out." Nate hastily piled the items he'd carried in just outside her apartment door, then gently nudged her and Lucy aside and pulled his weapon. Watching as he and Murphy crossed the threshold had her sending up another silent, desperate prayer.

Please, Lord, keep us all safe!

"Aunt Willow, you're messy like Mommy and Daddy," Lucy said, breaking into her thoughts.

The reminder of how much worse things could be helped calm her racing heart. She forced a smile, relieved that Lucy hadn't picked up on the sinister nature of their situation. "Yes, it sure looks that way."

"I'm hungry," Lucy complained.

Food wasn't even close to the top of her list, but she knew Lucy needed to eat dinner, especially since she highly doubted the little girl had eaten anything substantial for lunch. The burn of resentment hit hard, but she pushed it away. Alex and Debra were gone. Dead. Despite their neglect of Lucy, they certainly didn't deserve to be murdered.

Was it possible the same person who'd killed them had done this to her apartment? If so, why? Had they been searching for something? The same thing they hadn't found at Alex and Debra's?

She suppressed a shiver.

Glancing again at the mess, she swallowed hard. It was very tempting to ask Nate to drive her and Lucy to the nearest hotel. Especially considering the handle on her apartment door was broken.

"There's no one inside," Nate informed

her. "I'll call for a team to respond, although it seems unlikely we'll be able to lift any fingerprints. Whoever did this was likely smart enough to wear gloves."

The idea of more strangers invading her small apartment was unsettling. "Okay."

Nate's expression softened. "I'm sorry. I know you've already been through a lot. Whoever did this made a huge mess, but thankfully there isn't a lot of actual damage." He looked at her thoughtfully for a moment. "It seems the person responsible spent a lot of time going through your closet and dresser drawers as if searching for something."

The chill returned. "You think this is related to what happened to Alex and Debra?"

"Maybe, but I'm not convinced. You said yourself, your brother and sister-in-law weren't expecting you to visit. Then again, the timing is a strange coincidence." He frowned, thinking it through, then glanced at his watch. "The patrol officers should be here soon. Oh, and I'm sorry, but I need Lucy's bloodstained clothes for evidence."

She nodded, suppressing a shiver. Borrowing gloves from Nate, she carefully took the little girl's yellow outfit off, gingerly handing it to Nate, who placed it in an evidence bag. Stripping the gloves off, she dressed Lucy in a new pink outfit she'd purchased from the store. Sitting back against the wall, she wished she'd bought more snacks for Lucy. At this rate, the poor child would never get her dinner. She felt bad, as if she were no better at caring for Lucy than Alex and Debra had been.

The two officers arrived five minutes later. They disappeared inside her apartment with Nate and Murphy. Frustrated and exhausted, Willow sat on the floor in the hallway just outside her apartment next to Lucy. She pulled the baby doll she'd purchased at the store out of one of the bags and gave it to her niece. Together, they played with the doll, Willow doing whatever she could think of to keep the little girl occupied.

But she couldn't forget how her apartment had been thoroughly searched. Or the way her brother and his wife had been brutally murdered.

The fingerprint crew showed up a few minutes later, and it took them over an hour to check the various surfaces for prints.

"Willow?" Nate came out and hunkered down beside her. "We'll need your prints so we can exclude them from anything we may have found. The place was really very clean. There weren't many prints at all."

"Okay." She shifted Lucy off her lap. As she was about to stand, Nate held out his hand to her. After a moment's hesitation, she put her hand in his and allowed him to draw her upright. His warm palm was strangely reassuring. She wanted to cling to his strength but forced herself to let go.

"Thanks." She inwardly grimaced at her breathless tone. She really needed to get a hold of herself. This weird attraction she felt toward the K-9 cop was not healthy. She didn't have time for such nonsense.

Lucy was the only thing that mattered right now. Not her dearth of a love life. The little girl deserved a stable, loving home and

Willow planned to do whatever it took to provide that for her.

Once she'd been fingerprinted, the crime scene techs took off, leaving a mess of black fingerprint powder covering numerous surfaces behind.

Crazy to have spent the hour after Sunday services cleaning prior to heading over to confront her brother about Lucy. She'd need to clean, again.

"Here, let's get your stuff inside." Nate bent down to gather her bags. "We'll leave the car seat here for now. I'll need you to tell me if anything has been stolen."

Feeling nervous, she followed him into the apartment. The two officers who'd initially responded were standing off in the corner of her living room, speaking in low tones. Murphy brushed against her legs and she was oddly reassured when the animal stayed close.

She wiped the kitchen counter, then began unpacking the groceries. Nate went over to speak with the two officers. The task of putting her apartment back together seemed overwhelming, but what choice did she have? She was emotionally and physically exhausted. The last thing she wanted to do was pack up and move to a hotel. But staying here with a broken door handle wasn't a very good idea, either.

The two officers headed out of the apartment. She must have looked upset, because Nate crossed over to put a reassuring hand on her shoulder.

"They're not leaving, I just want them to check the video cameras for any footage of the person who did this."

"Oh." She tried to offer a smile. "That would be good, right? Then we'd know who murdered Alex and Debra."

"Only if these two crimes are linked," Nate cautioned. "Listen, I want to look around again and then will likely have some questions for you."

"Okay, but I need to feed Lucy something for dinner. She needs something more substantial than animal crackers in her belly."

"Understood." He gave her shoulder a reassuring squeeze, then moved away. She instantly missed the warmth of his touch.

She reminded herself that the men in her life didn't stick around. She'd dated a few, only to have them quickly disappear. Either because she wasn't very exciting or because she worked too many hours, or both.

Once the pizza was in the oven, she quickly wiped down the small kitchen table so Lucy would have a place to sit, then replaced her sofa cushions. She couldn't comprehend why anyone would be looking for something of Alex's in her apartment. Especially since she and Alex hadn't been close in a very long time.

Since before the death of their grandmother, three years ago, right after Lucy was born. They'd each received a modest inheritance; she'd invested hers in this apartment. When Alex and Debra had moved into their two-story, she'd praised him for putting his money to good use, only to have him laugh at her, carelessly announcing they were just renting the cheap place and living off the money and enjoying life. Despite having Lucy, Debra made it clear she wasn't interested in settling down.

Watching as Lucy played with her new baby doll, Willow tried to find the forgiveness in her heart that she knew God expected of her. Alex and Debra had gone down a bad path and unfortunately had paid the ultimate price.

Deep down, she knew they hadn't intentionally neglected Lucy. Despite Alex's being two years her senior, he was immature and irresponsible.

"Willow?"

Nate's deep voice startled her. "Yes?"

"Do you have a minute?"

"Sure." She peeked at the pizza through the glass oven door before hurrying to her master bedroom. "What is it?"

He gestured to a small slip of paper lying on the floor tucked beneath the open closet door. "That appears to be a cash receipt for gas. Is it yours?"

"Gas?" She dropped to her knees to see the receipt more clearly. "No." She glanced up at him. "I don't own a car. Why would I buy gas?"

"Yeah, that's what I thought." He pulled an evidence bag from the pocket of his uniform and used the plastic bag to cover his fingers as he carefully picked the receipt off the floor. The gas had been paid for with cash, and the identifying number across the top was smudged, but he thought Eden might be able to find the station. Maybe they'd discover there were cameras nearby.

Then he had another idea. After he had the slip of paper tucked inside the evidence bag, he called Murphy over and opened the bag for the K-9. "Seek, Murphy."

The yellow Lab buried his nose in the evidence bag, sniffing for what seemed like an inordinate amount of time.

"Seek," Nate repeated in a commanding tone.

Murphy put his snout to the floor and sniffed, breaking into a lope as he tracked the scent across the hardwood floor of her bedroom, through the doorway into the open-concept kitchen and living area. Then the dog headed for the door.

"Wait. Are you leaving us here alone?" She couldn't hide the underlying panic in her tone.

"No. Heel, Murphy." He paused and used his radio to call the two officers. "I need one or both of you to return to the apartment."

"Ten-four. We're on our way. The video isn't helpful anyway."

Once again, she tried to tell herself that the two cops were just as capable of protecting her and Lucy as Nate and Murphy.

But when they arrived and Nate took off with Murphy, she couldn't help feeling starkly alone.

Pumped with adrenaline at finally having a solid clue, Nate followed Murphy as the dog tracked the scent of the intruder down the hall toward the elevator. His partner made several twists and turns, but then pressed his nose against the narrow crack between the floor and the closed elevator doors.

Murphy stayed there for a long moment,

then made a circle in front of the elevator, returning to the closed doors for the second time. He sat, then gazed up at Nate with what he perceived as an imploring gaze.

"It's okay, boy. We're going to get him." Nate quickly clipped Murphy's leash to his collar, then pushed the button to summon the elevators. The one on the right opened first, and he held the door open. "Seek, Murphy."

The dog put his nose to the ground and took his time, but never alerted. Nate squelched a flash of concern. He decided since there were only two elevators, he'd head down to the lobby to see if Murphy could pick up the scent there.

Once they were in the lobby, it took another several minutes of sniffing and searching for Murphy to pick up the scent, near the second elevator. "Good boy," he praised, giving Murphy a good rub. "Seek!"

His partner gamely went back to work, sniffing and alerting again near the doorway heading outside. Nate knew that once they were out in the elements the scent may be more difficult to track. About a year and a half ago, the NYC K-9 Command Unit in Queens had been gifted a Labrador retriever named Stella from the Czech Republic. Stella had delivered eight puppies shortly upon her arrival to the US. Stella currently worked as a bomb-sniffing dog, and several of her puppies had turned into equally talented K-9 cops. Murphy was one of Stella's pups, earning a reputation for being one of the best trackers their Brooklyn unit had working for them. Still, there were a lot of people walking around, moving up and down the sidewalks, back and forth from subways and other buildings. Murphy was good, but it wouldn't be easy to pick out one specific scent against all others.

"Heel." He waited for Murphy to sit at his side before offering the evidence bag again. This time, he pulled out the orange ball he carried with him. Like most of their K-9s, Murphy was trained with a reward system that involved playing. Murphy's tail wagged with excitement when he saw the ball, and he quickly sniffed at the evidence bag, eager to get to work.

"Seek, Murphy." Nate slipped the ball back into his pocket.

Murphy put his nose to the ground, going back and forth as he searched for the scent. Nate stayed close, keeping the leash short so that they wouldn't trip any of the pedestrians passing by.

Murphy picked up the scent a few minutes later, alerting near the corner of the apartment building. Nate could imagine the guy pausing there for a moment, sweeping his gaze over the area to see if anyone noticed him.

"Good boy," he praised again. "Seek."

Murphy put his nose back to the sidewalk and took off in an eastern direction, which made sense as Bay Ridge overlooked the upper and lower bays of the Atlantic Ocean and connected to Staten Island via the Verrazzano-Narrows Bridge to the west.

Murphy took a winding path as he tracked the perp's scent. His K-9 paused at the intersection, then alerted again, staring north.

When the light changed, they crossed the street and Murphy picked up the scent once again. As they approached the entrance to the subway, Nate's hopes deflated. If the perp had taken one of the trains, they'd never find him. Sure, there were cameras, but he didn't have a clue who they were looking for or even a time frame of the vandalism.

Thankfully, Murphy alerted at the next intersection, too. Trying to quell the sense of excitement, Nate glanced around, taking note of their surroundings. There was a single long building housing a few shops and small restaurants with apartments located up above.

Was Murphy still on point? He trusted his K-9, but the streets were busy, and he knew the endless multitude of scents, from people, food and the ocean, could be confusing.

His stomach rumbled with hunger as he caught a whiff of hamburger grease, followed closely by the scent of hot dogs. He and Murphy crossed the street, and soon his partner once again alerted, indicating he'd picked up the scent.

"Good boy!" Nate knew he'd have to throw the ball for a long time once they were finished. The K-9 deserved a nice reward.

His partner alerted again, and then kept going, making Nate break into a jog to keep up. For whatever reason, it seemed the scent Murphy was following was stronger here. They turned right at the next corner, then Murphy abruptly came to a halt right outside the door to a small restaurant. The animal stared straight ahead as if he could see through the glass door to the inside where his potential quarry may be hiding in wait.

Nate took a step back to get a better look at the building. The sign above the door was done in bright red against a white background.

The Burgerteria.

In smaller letters beneath were the words *Gourmet Burgers Served Daily.*

Unfortunately, the place was closed for the day. Peering at the sign, it appeared the burger place closed early on Sundays, at 5:00 p.m. rather than the usual 11 p.m. on weekdays and midnight on Fridays and Saturdays.

Murphy continued sitting and staring at the door, his nostrils quivering. Nate stepped up beside him and cupped his hands around his face so he could see inside without the glare from the light.

The place was empty and amazingly clean. There were several small square tables surrounded by four chairs as well as a long counter against the farthest wall.

He tried to imagine why the perp had come here so soon after ransacking Willow's apartment. Simply because he was hungry?

No, more likely because he was meeting someone. Maybe the perp had been paid to do the job by someone else. Nate couldn't imagine why the same person who'd searched Willow's apartment would want her brother and sister-in-law dead. Murder was a far cry from simple burglary.

Other than the timing, there was nothing else to indicate the two crimes were related.

Especially considering the Emery murders had followed the same MO as the twenty-year-old McGregor murders, which he knew had hung like a black cloud over Bradley and Penny McGregor.

His gut told him these two events couldn't possibly be connected. As he was about to turn away, he saw a flash of movement out of the corner of his eye.

Someone was still inside!

FOUR

"Hey!" Nate rapped on the door, trying to get the guy's attention. "Police!"

Nothing.

"Open up! I want to talk to you!"

Still nothing. Peering through the window, Nate couldn't see the person inside any longer. Had he gone out the back?

"Come, Murphy." Nate whirled away from the glass door and quickly walked along the sidewalk, looking for the quickest way to get to the back of the long building.

When he found a narrow walkway between the one structure and the next, he didn't hesitate to enter. There was just enough room for Murphy to walk alongside him. As they approached the back of the building, he slowed, straining to listen.

He didn't hear anything above the routine traffic, subway train and pedestrian noise.

Murphy stood beside him, nose in the air as if still seeking the scent from the gas receipt. His partner didn't alert, so Nate crept around the corner, keeping his back pressed against the wall.

The alley was long, stretching the entire length of the building. Several dumpsters were stationed at intervals along the way. He moved from dumpster to dumpster, wrinkling his nose at the pungent scent, searching for signs of someone hiding out.

He found what appeared to be the back door to the Burgerteria, but it was locked. He looked down at Murphy. "What do you think?"

The K-9 gazed up at him, waiting for the next command.

Nate offered the evidence bag to Murphy. "Seek."

Murphy eagerly sniffed the inside of the bag, then went to work along the alley. Nate kept one eye on Murphy, the other sweeping the area for any sign of danger.

Murphy scouted the area for several long minutes, but never alerted. Fifteen minutes later, Nate called him off.

"Heel, Murphy. Good boy." He rubbed the Lab's sleek coat, smiling as Murphy wiggled with joy and reminded himself he needed to take time to throw the K-9's orange ball.

"Come." He shortened Murphy's leash and returned through the narrow walkway to the street where the dog had last alerted on the intruder's scent. The Burgerteria was the only clue he had so far, other than the gas receipt itself, and he didn't like the fact that so far, both had led to a dead end. Maybe Eden could get more info from the receipt.

He headed back toward Willow's apartment building, wondering again if the perp had gone to the restaurant for a meal or to meet someone?

And if it was the latter, why? What could they have possibly been looking for inside Willow's apartment?

Nate always liked a puzzle, but this one bothered him more than most. Maybe because Willow was a beautiful woman alone caring for her young niece.

Before he reached Willow's apartment building, his phone rang. "Hey, Gavin, what's up?"

"Emergency staff meeting. Can you get here ASAP?"

He thought about the cops he had watching over Willow and Lucy. "Yeah, sure. I'm only a few minutes away."

The Brooklyn K-9 Unit headquarters was housed in a three-story limestone building that was a former police precinct until the unit merged with another precinct. Their new K-9 unit gladly took the abandoned space, making it their new home. A K-9 center with an outdoor training yard was located right next door, perfectly fitting in with room to grow.

Nate and Murphy made it to headquarters in record time. After entering the building, he nodded at Penelope McGregor, their desk clerk. Tall and slender with long red hair and dark brown eyes, Penny was only twenty-four, and the entire unit was protective of her. No one as much as her brother, Detective Bradley McGregor. “Hey, Penny, how are you holding up?”

She shrugged and grimaced. “It’s been horrible. I’m still reeling from this latest murder. Sarge asked me to attend the staff meeting with the rest of you.”

“Good.” Nate waved his hand toward the hallway. “Let’s go.”

He placed Murphy in one of the kennels kept in the precinct for just this reason, then followed Penny into the large conference room. The rest of the team was already assembled. The four female K-9 officers—Lani Jameson, who’d transferred from the NYC K-9 Command Unit after Gavin’s promotion, Belle Montera, Vivienne Armstrong and their newest rookie, Noelle Orton—were seated in a cluster, leaving the guys, Ray Morrow, Jackson Davison, Tyler Walker, Maxwell Santelli, Henry Roarke and Bradley McGregor, to fill in the other seats. Nate slid in next to Henry, while Penny took a seat beside her brother.

“Thanks for coming together late in the

day on short notice." Gavin Sutherland swept a serious gaze over his team. "As you may have heard, a married couple in East Flatbush, Alex and Debra Emery, were murdered earlier today. Thankfully, their three-year-old daughter, Lucy, a witness, was spared."

"Just like me," Penny whispered.

Gavin nodded. "Yes. The MO of the Emery murders is far too similar to your parents' case."

"The murderer, wearing a clown face with blue hair on top, entered the front yard, gave a stuffed monkey to Lucy, then shot both the Emerys in the back." Nate glanced at his colleagues. "Every detail the same as the McGregor murders twenty years ago, down to the exact same date."

"We've always known my parents' murderer is still out there, but why would he strike again now, after all these years?" Brad asked.

"We have to keep an open mind," Gavin cautioned. "But it's possible the perp was locked up at some point, for some other crime, and recently got out. Once the forensic specialist gets through the evidence, we may have more to go on." Gavin looked at his whole team. "I need all of you to work together on this. To back each other up in every way possible."

"We will." Nate infused confidence in his tone, and several of the other team members nodded their heads in agreement.

"Any news on Liberty?" Noelle Orton was paired with the beautiful yellow Lab, who they recently learned had a ten grand price placed on her head from a high-ranking gun runner. Liberty had foiled two military weapon smuggling operations in the past two months, so the kingpin wanted her and her skills out of the police business. The talented Lab was costing the gun runners way too much. Unfortunately, the dark smudge on Liberty's left ear made her far too easy to spot, so Gavin asked them all to be vigilant about watching for any strike against the K-9.

"No, unfortunately Liberty remains a target with a bounty on her head," Gavin said grimly. "You and Liberty need to continue keeping a low profile."

"Yes, sir." Noelle tried to hide her dejection, but everyone knew the rookie couldn't very well prove herself if she and her K-9 partner weren't allowed to work big cases.

Nate subtly glanced at his watch. Willow would be wondering where he was if they didn't finish up soon.

As if on cue, Gavin waved a hand. "That's all I have for now. Just be careful out there, okay?"

A chorus of "We will" echoed from the team members around the room.

Normally Nate would have lingered to chat with the rest of the team, heading over to the 646 Diner where they often went for a quick meal after work. But he needed to get back to Willow and Lucy, so he released Murphy from his kennel and left.

As he entered Willow's apartment building, he thought about Gavin's staff meeting and what he'd seen at the Burgerteria. He made a silent promise to get to the bottom of what was going on with Willow, even while continuing to investigate the Emery murders and the obvious link to the twenty-year-old McGregor case.

Willow tried to ignore her discomfort with the two uniformed officers standing outside her broken apartment door as she watched Lucy eat.

Voices from the hallway caught her attention.

“Thanks for staying.” Nate’s deep tone rippled through her, instantly relaxing her tense muscles. “I’ll take it from here.”

“Call if you need anything. We’ll be on duty until eleven.”

“I will.”

Turning toward the doorway, she met Nate’s gaze. “Well? You were gone for a long time. Did you and Murphy find anything?”

“Maybe.” He entered the apartment, two silver dog dishes tucked under one arm and a container of kibble in hand. He closed the door behind Murphy, even though it didn’t latch because the handle was broken. The yellow Lab took a seat in the center of her small kitchen, waiting as Nate filled one of the bowls with water, the other with dog food.

Murphy lapped up the water, then began to eat.

Nate watched his partner for a few minutes before turning toward her. "Murphy followed the scent from here all the way to the Burgerteria restaurant. Could be a simple coincidence, but my gut tells me the person who did this—" he waved a hand to indicate the mostly cleaned-up apartment "—was meeting someone there."

"The Burgerteria?" She drew her gaze from Murphy, grappling with the idea of the vandal going to the restaurant. "That's where I work as a line cook."

Nate's gaze sharpened. "For how long?"

"Three years, since I moved into this apartment." She thought it was strange that the vandal would go there. "Are you sure Murphy didn't follow my scent instead of the receipt?"

Nate's eyes darkened. "I'm positive. He's one of the best trackers we have."

She wanted to believe him, but it wasn't

easy. Why would the vandal go there? Sure, the place was only a few blocks away, and served great food, if she said so herself, but still.

"Aunt Willow? Are we safe now?" Lucy's tone drew her from her thoughts.

She did not want Lucy listening to their conversation. "Of course. Everything is going to be fine now. Where's your dolly?"

"Baby!" Lucy ran over to pick up her baby doll from the sofa, clutching it to her chest. Nate took off Murphy's vest and leash, and the lab went over to sniff at Lucy, then licked her. Lucy giggled but held the doll out of Murphy's reach, as if the K-9 might steal her. "My baby."

"Yes, she's your baby. Why don't you play in my room?" Willow smiled at her niece. "Maybe your baby needs a bottle?"

"Yes! She must be hungry." Lucy disappeared into the bedroom. Murphy followed, but then turned around and stretched out in front of the bedroom doorway. She watched him, touched by the way he was clearly protecting the little girl.

"Is there any reason someone at the Burgerteria would come here to search your place?" Nate's voice brought her back to the issue at hand. "Anyone carrying a grudge against you for some reason? Or have reason to believe you're hiding something?"

She let out an exasperated sigh. "Why would they? I make hundreds of gourmet burgers every day. I can't imagine why on earth that could possibly make someone upset with me. Or think that I would have something they'd want."

"Not sure." Nate glanced around, as if searching the apartment for answers. "It just seems like an odd coincidence that your place was tossed by someone who immediately left and went to the restaurant."

"A coincidence?" Her annoyance grew. "You mean like the fact that my apartment was broken into and searched the same day my brother and his wife were murdered? That kind of coincidence?"

"Easy, now. I told you, I'm not sure the two cases are related." Nate's attempt to calm her wasn't working.

"Well, it seems logical to me, that if anyone was looking for me, they'd know to come to the Burgerteria. They wouldn't have to come here to search my place. I don't have anything here." She was tired and cranky but knew it wasn't Nate's fault. He was only trying to help.

It was all just too much.

Her stomach rumbled, and she blew out a breath and gestured toward the pizza. "Are you hungry? We can share what's left."

"I could eat." Nate stepped toward her, his blue eyes searching hers. "Willow, I know you've had a long day. I'm just trying to understand what's going on."

"I know." His gentleness was nearly her undoing. Tears threatened, and she bit her lip and pinched the bridge of her nose to ward them off. She couldn't afford to break down. Not with Lucy in the next room. She drew in a deep breath. "I— Thank you, Nate. I appreciate everything you've done for us."

"Sit down." He put a hand on the small

of her back and steered her toward a chair. "I'll dish up the pizza."

She dropped into the seat and sighed. "It's probably cold."

"I love cold pizza."

His comment made her smile. Talk about being willing to look on the bright side of things. She watched as he went to the counter and opened cupboards until he found plates and glasses. After piling two slices of pizza on each plate, he brought them over. "Milk? Or water?"

"Milk is fine. We may as well drink it up. I bought it for Lucy, but she doesn't seem to care for it much."

"Maybe she hasn't been exposed to it enough." Nate filled two glasses with milk and set them on the table. "Give her some time. She'll get used to it."

She thought about how her brother's kitchen had looked, with the dirty dishes, trash and empty liquor bottles strewn about. "You're probably right. I'm afraid that little girl is going to need a lot of time to adjust to her new life. And to the loss of her parents."

Nate reached over to squeeze her hand. “I’m glad she has you.”

The stupid tears burned again, but she summoned a smile. “We have each other.”

They finished the rest of their pizza in silence. She felt herself blush when Nate’s gaze lingered on her features and she wondered if she had smears of pizza sauce on her face. She wiped at her mouth and pushed her plate away. “You can have the rest, if you like. I’m full.”

“Sure?” Nate’s gaze was hopeful.

“Yes. It’s the least I can do.” She frowned and glanced at her door. It bothered her that the door handle was still broken, but she didn’t have a clue how to replace it. “Do you think we should move into a hotel for the night?”

Nate followed her gaze and she wondered what he was thinking. He cleared his throat. “I have a better idea. Murphy and I will bunk here for the night.”

“Here?” Her voice squeaked. “There’s not enough room.”

He shrugged. "I'll sleep on the sofa. Murphy doesn't mind the floor."

"The sofa?" She knew she sounded like a parrot repeating everything back to him. She didn't want to be alone, but the idea of sharing her small apartment was a bit distracting. "Are you sure?"

"Absolutely." He smiled and she had to cross her arms over her chest to keep from hugging him.

She probably wouldn't sleep much anyway, but knowing Nate Slater and Murphy were here to protect them gave her the sense of peace she desperately needed.

As Willow spread a sheet over the sofa and added a blanket and pillow, he found himself wondering if he'd lost his mind.

Everything about Willow Emery screamed happy homemaker. She was a nurturer, a nester.

She was everything he knew he couldn't have.

"If you need anything else, just holler."

Her smile was sweet. "Thanks again for doing this."

He cleared his throat, pulling himself together with an effort. "You're welcome. Listen, I have to take Murphy outside one last time, but I won't go far. I'll keep my eye on the front of the building at all times."

A flash of alarm rippled across her features, but she nodded. "Okay."

He pulled out his cell phone and swiped at his screen, then met her gaze. "Tell me your number."

She recited the number. He punched it in, then he called her phone. The screen lit up and the phone chirped. "There, now you have my number, too. I promise, it won't take long."

She went over and scooped up her phone. "Thank you."

He nodded, then placed Murphy's vest on, and clipped the leash to his collar. "We'll be back soon."

He took Murphy down to the lobby. There was a small patch of grass that wasn't far from Willow's redbrick building. Once

Murphy did his thing, Nate cleaned up after him, then tossed the orange ball, keeping his eye on the front door of Willow's building. Several people entered, but no one looked suspicious.

His phone remained reassuringly silent.

The puzzle pieces surrounding the case filtered through his mind. The perp had gone from Willow's apartment to the Burgerteria where she worked. To meet someone? It was the only thing that made sense.

Yet Willow had a point about how anyone looking for her would know when she was working. Why break into her apartment to search for something today, a day she had off work? Why not pick a day she was working late instead?

All good questions without the barest hint of an answer.

Ten minutes later, he bent over to rub Murphy, deciding he'd given the K-9 enough attention for now. He pocketed the orange ball and took Murphy back inside, riding the elevator to the seventh floor. He approached Willow's broken door, then dropped to one knee to examine the handle more closely. It would need to be replaced, something he could do for her in the morning.

After heading into the apartment, he closed the door and pressed one of the kitchen chairs firmly up against it. Murphy would let him know before anyone got close, but he figured the added barrier couldn't hurt.

Murphy lapped water from his bowl. As Nate went past the bedroom door, he heard Willow and Lucy talking.

"It's time to say our bedtime prayers," Willow said.

"What are bedtime prayers?"

"I'll show you. First you need to be tucked in underneath the covers." There was a rustle of sheets as Lucy complied. "Now put your hands together like this and close your eyes."

"Okay."

"Dear Lord, we ask You to bless Nate and Murphy, for everything they've done for us today. We also ask You to watch over us as we sleep, keeping us safe from harm. Amen."

There was a pause, before Willow added, "Lucy, you need to say amen, too."

"Oh. Amen."

"Good. Now we can go to sleep, knowing that we'll be safe in God's care."

Nate backed away from the door. The idea of praying like that was completely foreign to him.

For a moment he remembered the night his father had lost all semblance of control. The way the old man had lashed out, hitting his mother so hard she flew halfway across the room. The way he'd rushed his father, his skinny ten-year-old fists hitting his father's belly, bouncing off harmlessly as he begged him to stop.

The way his father had backhanded him, pain blooming in his head as he crashed into the wall, falling to the floor in a crumpled heap.

Sweat popped out on his forehead, the back of his throat burning from pent-up screams locked in his mind. With an effort, he forced the twenty-year-old images away. Turning away from the door, he went over to stretch out on the sofa. Murphy plopped on the floor next to him.

He reached down to rest his hand on Murphy's soft fur. His partner was real. Murphy would do whatever was necessary to protect him and the woman and child in the next room.

No, he didn't believe for one moment that God had ever watched over him.

FIVE

Lucy had woken up twice during the night, each time crying over the bad clown with blue hair. Willow's heart ached for the little girl and she had cuddled her close, rocking her back to sleep.

Finally, they'd both slept. When daylight filtered past the window shades, Willow awoke, staring at the ceiling fan overhead. She prayed that God would guide her in being a good aunt to Lucy, and for God to provide comfort to the little girl as she struggled through this difficult time.

Feeling at peace, she slid from bed, trying not to wake Lucy. But her niece must have sensed her absence, as she almost instantly opened her eyes. "Aunt Willow? Where are you going?"

"I'm not leaving, I'm just going to the kitchen to make breakfast. Are you hungry?"

Lucy rubbed her eyes and nodded. She pushed her hair from her face and popped up from the bed.

Willow led Lucy out to the kitchen. The little girl remained glued to her side, and she knew her niece was strongly feeling the impact of yesterday's events.

And likely would for a long time to come.

Murphy came over, his tail wagging in greeting.

"Hey, Murphy." Willow stroked his soft fur and scratched him behind the ears. "You're a good boy, aren't you?"

Murphy licked her, his entire body wiggling with happiness.

Lucy wrapped her arms around Murphy's neck, pressing her face to his fur. "I love Murphy."

"I know you do." It was clear that having Murphy around was good for Lucy's emotional well-being. She glanced at the living room sofa. Nate's lean body was still supine on the sofa, but he was awake, blinking sleep from his eyes, looking adorably rumpled with his bedhead and shadowed jaw. She felt her cheeks grow warm and hoped he didn't notice her embarrassment. "Good morning, Nate."

"Morning." He yawned and rolled into a sitting position, rubbing his hand against his jaw. "Did you sleep okay?"

"So-so." She didn't want to remind Lucy about the nightmares. She noticed the chair pushed up against the door, and was grateful Nate had agreed to stay.

As if he'd noticed her gaze, he gestured toward the door. "I need to take Murphy outside, but afterward, I'll work on replacing your door handle."

"Thanks. Lucy is hungry and so am I, so I'm going to make breakfast for all of us." She glanced down at Lucy. "Do you like scrambled eggs and toast?"

Lucy tipped her head to the side, her brow puckered in a frown. "I don't know."

Her heart ached for the little girl.

"I love scrambled eggs and toast." Nate's assertion caught Lucy's attention.

"You do?" Lucy looked up at him curiously.

"Absolutely. They're my favorite." Willow thought he might be exaggerating about that just a bit but appreciated his help.

"Will you give them a try?" Willow smiled down at Lucy.

"Okay."

"Would you like to help me cook the eggs, Lucy?"

Lucy nodded and she took the little girl over to the counter. She pulled over a chair and helped Lucy stand on the seat so she could reach. As Willow broke a half dozen eggs in a bowl and showed her niece how to whisk them together, Nate took Murphy outside.

When Nate and Murphy returned, the eggs and several slices of toast were finished. She set the plates on the table, bringing the chair back over for Lucy to sit in.

Lucy looked at the eggs with suspicion, but as Nate eagerly dived into his meal, she gamely tried hers. Her face broke into a grin. "These are yummy, Aunt Willow."

"Thank you." She was relieved Lucy liked them. "It was nice of you to help me make them."

"It was fun." Lucy ate another bite of her eggs.

"Thanks for breakfast. As soon as I'm finished here, I'll work on your door," Nate promised.

"That would be great." She knew, though, that just having a locked door wasn't going to make her feel safe. It was having Nate and Murphy here overnight that had given her peace of mind.

But she also knew they couldn't stay forever.

"Do you have to work today?" She glanced at Nate.

"Yes, but I can go in a little later than usual. I told Sarge I'll be a bit late, and he understood."

She remembered the conversation with his boss when they'd discussed Alex's and Debra's murders as potentially being committed by some sort of serial killer on the loose. But before she could ask him about it, Lucy spoke up.

"Are Mommy and Daddy coming to get me?"

She froze, giving Nate a panicked look. He frowned and offered a helpless shrug. She carefully set her fork down, searching for the best way to approach the subject of death and dying with her niece. Finally, she curled her arm around the little girl's shoulders. "No, sweetie, I'm afraid not."

She fully expected Lucy to ask more questions, but the little girl seemed to accept her answer.

For now.

Lucy pressed her face into Willow's chest. She held her niece for a long moment, silently praying for God to help the little girl get through this.

Nate's empathetic expression was touching. After a few moments, he cleared his throat. "Lucy, after you finish breakfast, would you mind playing with Murphy? I think he feels a little lonely."

Intrigued, Lucy lifted her head. "Really?"

"Really." Nate finished his toast and eggs, then stood to carry his plate to the kitchen sink. "Willow, do you have a screwdriver?"

"Yes." She went into her closet to pull out a small tool kit. "I have all the basics here."

"Nice. The handle is broken, so I'll need to find replacement parts or buy a new one."

Lucy finished her breakfast, then scampered down off the booster seat to play with Murphy. The yellow Lab was exceptionally patient with the little girl, as if sensing his role was not only to protect her, but to keep her occupied.

"I'll call a friend to pick up a new door handle."

Willow nodded, turning her attention to household chores. When Nate had the new handle, he went back to work on the door. She liked listening to him whistle under his breath as he worked. It was nice having him around, but she knew that once he'd finished his task, he and Murphy would need to leave.

Their boss was waiting for them.

Speaking of which, she abruptly glanced

at the clock. Nine forty-five in the morning. Oops. She'd completely forgotten to call her boss to let him know she wouldn't be in. She originally had planned to use the Nanna's Nook Day Care for Lucy while she worked, if she'd been able to convince Alex and Debra to let her take Lucy, but after everything that had happened, she didn't want to leave the little girl alone.

The restaurant opened at ten thirty in the morning, but she normally arrived an hour before. She picked up her phone and called the Burgerteria. "Damon? It's Willow. I'm sorry, but I'm not going to make it in to work today."

"What?" The outrage in his voice made her wince. "I need you. You're supposed to be here right now prepping for the lunch crowd!"

"I know, I'm sorry. But my brother and his wife were murdered yesterday, and I have my three-year-old niece here. I can't leave her alone."

"I'm sorry about that, but I don't have anyone to replace you." The anger faded from his tone. "Isn't there any way you can make it in?"

She glanced at Nate, who was clearly listening to her side of the conversation, a frown puckering his brow. "I'm sorry, but I can't leave Lucy. In fact, based on the long hours I normally have to work it may be better for me to give my notice."

"You're quitting?" Damon let out a harsh laugh. "Fine. Have it your way."

The connection went dead.

"Well. I guess that's that." Willow set her phone on the counter, a hollow feeling in her chest. While she knew that this was the best thing for Lucy right now, it didn't sit right to be completely out of a job.

She had some money saved up, but it wouldn't last forever. She'd need some sort of employment, something that would help support Lucy while offering some flexibility of hours.

Doing what, exactly? She had no clue.

Nate couldn't deny being relieved that Willow had quit her job at the Burgerteria, as he didn't like how Murphy had followed the intruder's scent to the place. Yet, the forlorn expression on her face bothered him.

"Are you okay?" Now that her apartment door handle was replaced, the lock secure, he moved closer to her. He rested a hand on her slim shoulder.

"I will be." She put on a brave smile. "Damon isn't happy with me, but I know it's the right thing to do, for Lucy's sake."

He searched her gaze. "And you're absolutely sure your boss doesn't have a reason to be upset with you?"

"You mean other than quitting my job?" There was a brittle edge to her tone.

The break-in had happened while she'd been in East Flatbush. Before the murders? Or afterward? He wished he knew for certain.

"Yes, I mean prior to today. Was your boss unhappy with your work performance for any reason?"

"Not that I'm aware of. In fact, he'd just asked me to take photos for the new menu."

He raised a brow. "I'm surprised he didn't hire a professional photographer."

She snorted. "No way. Do you have any idea how much that would cost? I'm in a photography class, and did a decent job photographing the various types of gourmet burgers, if I say so myself."

"I'd like to see them." He didn't see how pictures of burgers could play into this, but the intruder *had* gone to the Burgerteria after ransacking her home, and there had to be some connection. Plus, maybe he was also just a little curious to see her work. For some strange reason, Willow Emery intrigued him. Not just because she'd taken her niece in without a moment's hesitation, but because she was beautiful and smart. Because of the way she'd kept her cool under pressure in the aftermath of violence, while displaying a softer, gentler side toward her niece.

She was a bit of an enigma, but he couldn't afford to get emotionally involved.

"My camera is in my bag. I tend to carry it wherever I go." Willow opened the oversize bag he recognized from the day before. She pulled out a midsize digital camera and turned it around so he could see the screen.

"That's a pretty nice camera." Nate looked impressed.

"Didn't cost as much as you might think. I bought it at the new discount store that opened recently, Basement Bargains." She tapped the screen. "See? Dozens of pictures of burgers."

He had to admit they were good photos. She'd done a good job of getting the correct angle, displaying the burger in a way that emphasized what toppings were included. Anything from the traditional mushroom and swiss cheese to avocado and alfalfa sprouts.

"Did you use these for your class?"

"Yes, among others." She took the camera and flipped through the photos. She hadn't been kidding—there were well over three dozen hamburger photos. "I added a few with people, too. A few at the restaurant but more at the park."

He recognized Owl's Head Park and appreciated how she'd chosen interesting people to photograph. An older woman sitting with a large bag at her feet, two young kids chasing each other, a young man resting with his head back, eyes closed. He went back to the photos at the Burgerteria and found one with two men talking to each other.

"Who are these guys?" He held the camera toward her.

She pointed toward the younger of the two men. "This one is Damon Berk, the restaurant manager. I don't know who the other man is. I only photographed him because of his craggy face. It was so unique, I wanted to capture it."

He couldn't deny she was right about Craggy Face. His cheeks were lined and loose, yet his cheekbones were prominent, reminding him of twin mountain peaks overlooking a crevasse.

He thought back to the shadow he'd noticed in the back of the restaurant last evening. Had Damon Berk been back there? As the manager it made sense, but he couldn't be sure.

"My photography instructor loved that one, asked me to print a copy for the rest of the class to see." Willow's voice brought him back to the present.

He jerked his gaze to hers. "You sent it via email? I'd like to see it up close."

"Of course." She went over and pulled a small notebook computer from her bag. "The battery is low. Give me a moment to power it up."

While she plugged in the computer, he noticed Lucy had tied her doll's bonnet on Murphy's head. It was a testament to his training that Murphy didn't go nuts trying to rip it off. Murphy thumped his tail, his large brown eyes looking up at Nate as if saying, *hey, whatever makes her happy.*

"You're a good boy," he praised.

Murphy came over, tail wagging. Lucy followed, clutching her baby doll to her chest. "Isn't Murphy cute?"

"He sure is." His lips twitched at Murphy's bonnet. "Willow, you should take a picture of this."

She turned from her computer and picked up the camera. As if sensing he was the subject of the photo, Murphy looked away.

It took several attempts, and Willow was chuckling by the time she was finished. "So typical, takes twenty attempts to get one decent shot."

He leaned forward to see the screen. "It's great."

Lucy went back to the sofa, still talking to her baby doll. It occurred to Nate that she needed more things to play with and he made a mental note to find out how soon the crime scene would be cleared so Willow could pick up more of Lucy's things.

"Okay, here's the picture of Damon with the man at Burgerteria." Willow turned the computer screen so he could see it better. "I did make a few changes, but this one was my favorite. Blurring out the background helped make his features stand out more."

"It sure does." He stared at the craggy face, committing it to memory. Then he was struck by an idea. “Hey, can you print this one for me? I might be able to put his face through our database to find his name.”

“I don’t have a printer here. I use the one at school. They let us print for free as long as we purchase the photo paper.” She snapped her fingers and rose to her feet. “Wait, I printed extra copies for myself. I’m happy to give you one. The photograph will be better quality than via text message or email.”

“Great, thanks. Although I wouldn’t mind if you texted me the picture of Murphy.”

She glanced at him in surprise, then nodded. “Of course.”

Nate knew there was no proof that Craggy Face had anything to do with ransacking her home, but he figured it couldn’t hurt to ID the guy. Especially since Murphy trailed the intruder’s scent directly to the Burgerteria.

Willow opened several drawers of the narrow desk set in the corner of the living room. “I don’t understand. I thought for sure I left the photos in here.”

The back of his neck prickled in warning, and he shot to his feet. “Those drawers were open when you came in last night, weren't they?"

Willow straightened, her expression full of concern. "Yes." She glanced back down at the drawer. "I know for sure the photos were in a brown envelope tucked into this top wide drawer. They were too big to fit in the narrower ones along the side."

Nate crossed over to join her. In his mind's eye he remembered how the closet and bedroom drawers were opened and searched, along with the couch cushions being on the floor, and then this desk, with the drawer left open. The rest of the living room and kitchen had been basically untouched.

Because the intruder had found exactly what he'd been searching for.

Willow's photographs.

SIX

Her pictures had been stolen. Willow stared down at the empty drawer, trying to wrap her mind around what had happened. None of it made any sense. "They searched my apartment just for the photos?"

"Looks that way to me." Nate lightly rested his hand in the center of her back. "I have to believe the person who did this really wanted that photo of the craggy-faced man. Are you sure you don't know who he is?"

She lifted her shoulders in a helpless shrug. "I'm sure. Damon never introduced him to me, so he must not be involved in running the place."

Nate's blue eyes flashed with interest. "You've seen him before? He's a regular at the restaurant?"

Clearly this was important, so she tried to

think back to the day she'd done the hamburger photos. Craggy Face had been there that day, but she hadn't really paid attention to him, or to Damon for that matter. Her focus was on getting the best pictures possible for the menu. The better the restaurant did, the more job security for her.

At least, that had been her thought at the time.

Had she seen Craggy Face before that day? Her mind was nothing but a jumble of bits and pieces of memories. She honestly couldn't say.

"I'm sorry." She hated feeling as if she were letting Nate down. "I don't remember if he had been around the restaurant before or not. It's possible. The only thing I can say for certain is that he's not a regular."

Nate offered a crooked smile. "Don't apologize. It's my job to ask difficult questions. I guess it's good to know he isn't a regular. But I'd really like to know who he is. Seems like he must be a significant piece of the puzzle."

His words hit square in the gut, and she

sank to the edge of her sofa. "You were right. This break-in wasn't related to Alex and Debra's murder."

"Yes, that's my take on the issue." His tone was gentle and he came over to sit beside her. His musky scent soothed her frayed nerves and she tried not to think about what it would be like to be in the apartment without him and Murphy standing guard. "Something is up with your boss and that guy in the photo. Bad enough to break into your house to get their hands on the picture. I'm sure they believe you deleted them from your camera, but regardless, I'm glad you quit your job, Willow. You need to stay far away from your boss and the restaurant."

She sighed. "I won't miss the long hours, especially now that I have Lucy, but the pay was decent. I'll need to find another job, hopefully one with flexibility."

His brow furrowed. "Do you need extra money? I can lend you some..."

"What? No!" She jumped up, horrified by his offer. "I'll be fine for a while. I just can't live off my savings forever."

"Okay, but don't hesitate to call me if you need something."

She wouldn't, but it was a kind gesture. She had to call Nanna's Nook to let them know she may not be bringing Lucy in for a few days. Maybe they'd let her postpone a week or so without charging her. Hopefully by then she'd have at least a part-time job.

She wished she could make a living as a photographer; the hours would be extremely flexible. Yet she knew that while it was a great hobby, she wasn't good enough to bring in a steady income.

Nate's phone chirped and he abruptly rose to his feet. "Excuse me." He moved toward the kitchen. "Hey, Sarge, I have a name I need you to run through the system. Damon Berk, manager of the Burgerteria."

As Nate moved into the corner of the room to discuss her current situation with his boss, she went over to her computer and went to a job search website. Since her recent experience was in the restaurant business, she narrowed her search to similar types of jobs within a five-mile radius.

She recognized the Sunshine Sidewalk Café, a small but nice place that happened to be located a couple of blocks from her apartment, in the opposite direction from the Burgerteria. The café was advertising for a server position, and while she would prefer to be a cook, the hours as a server at the café might be better for child care.

She glanced over at Lucy. Her niece was stretched out on the floor next to Murphy, talking to herself as she rested her head on his torso. Her blond tresses were nearly the same color as Murphy's silky coat. Seeing the two of them together had her reaching for her camera.

This time, Murphy didn't move from his position, almost as if he didn't want to disturb the little girl. She took several cute photos, wondering what steps she'd need to take in order to become Lucy's legal guardian. So much had happened yesterday that she hadn't given the legalities of her new situation much consideration.

She made a mental note to check in with Child Protective Services to find out. But then it occurred to her that not having even a part-time job may actually be a black mark against her.

Setting her camera aside, she went back to the job site and clicked the link to submit her résumé.

Nate returned and she caught the last part of his conversation. "Yes, Lucy is our only witness to the Emery murders. Staying here on protective detail for a bit is good, but I need to work the case, too. Finding and arresting this guy is important to me. Especially given the link to the McGregor murders."

She remembered he'd said something about her brother's murder being similar to a previous murder. Was that why he'd seemed so struck by Lucy's description? She couldn't help looking directly at Nate as he disconnected from the call.

"Any clues?"

"Not yet. Damon Berk is clean, no criminal record."

She wasn't surprised. "He's a very busy restaurant manager. I can't even imagine he'd have time to be involved with any criminal activity."

"You never know." Nate cleared his throat. "I hope you don't mind, Willow, but Murphy and I are going to stick around for a couple of days. I promise we won't be any trouble."

"Of course I don't mind. Having you and Murphy stay is no problem at all." She hoped he didn't sense just how happy she was to hear the news.

As much as she knew she needed to be careful not to get too emotionally involved with the handsome K-9 cop, she couldn't deny the overwhelming wave of relief that he and Murphy weren't leaving anytime soon.

Frustrating that Damon Berk didn't have a rap sheet. The more Nate thought about it, the more he believed Craggy Face was the key.

"Listen, Sarge wants you and Lucy to come in for a formal interview."

Willow frowned, glancing at Lucy.

"Today? I don't know…she woke twice last night with bad nightmares."

It was troubling to hear Lucy was suffering from nightmares, but she was their only witness to a crime that could help solve a twenty-year-old murder, as well as this current one. "I know. But I wouldn't ask if it wasn't important."

A resigned expression crossed her features. "Okay, fine. But I want to make a quick stop along the way."

He tensed. "What kind of stop?"

"The Sunshine Sidewalk Café has a job opening." She gestured toward her computer. "I want to check the place out."

He resisted the urge to yank at his hair and kept his tone even with an effort. "This isn't a good time to get a new job, Willow."

"It's not like I'm going to start a new job today." She closed her computer with a snap. "I'm sure I can start in a week or so, once the danger is over."

He didn't like it but figured a quick stop couldn't hurt. As Willow helped Lucy get ready to go, he thought about his conversation with Gavin. Damon Berk had been a dead end, but they had a new line to tug on. Gavin had told him how neighborhood interviews revealed the Emerys weren't well-liked because of their party lifestyle, their messy home and the way they often ignored Lucy. Apparently, several neighbors had been concerned about the girl playing outside alone. Even more importantly, they hadn't paid their rent for the past five months. Late notices and potential eviction warnings had been ignored. The owners of the duplex were a married couple by the name of Mike and Liz O'Malley. Gavin had put their tech guru, Eden Chang, on task to track them down.

It seemed extreme to believe a property landlord would stoop to murder—and borrow from the MO of a cold case—in order to get rid of a couple of deadbeat tenants, but stranger things had happened, and he knew every possibility, no matter how remote, couldn't be ignored. They'd need to verify the O'Malleys' alibi, if they had one, in order to cross them off the suspect list.

He kept coming back to the similarities between the Emery murders and the twenty-year-old cold case. The exact same day, clown mask with blue hair, dressed in black and the stuffed monkey.

Leaving a small child alive, despite being a potential witness.

Why use the same MO? What did it mean?

"I think we're finally ready."

Willow's voice cut into his thoughts. He turned to find Lucy strapped into a lightweight stroller, clutching her baby doll. They were so cute, his heart gave a betraying thump of awareness in his chest.

"Guess I'm lagging behind. Come, Murphy." His partner came to his side. He pulled Murphy's vest on, then clipped a leash to his collar. Murphy instantly straightened, his nose working as he understood he was now on duty. "Do you have everything you need?"

Willow looped her bag over her shoulder. "I think so."

"All right, let's go."

"I hope you don't mind walking to the café." Willow pushed Lucy's stroller into the hallway, then locked the apartment door, stuffing the key into her large bag. "It's only three blocks away."

Murphy needed exercise, so he nodded. "Not a problem. But we'll need to take the SUV to headquarters."

She stopped in front of the elevator. "Good thing we left Lucy's car seat in your vehicle."

He smiled and nodded. "I know."

The elevator doors opened. Willow pushed Lucy's stroller inside, turning around so she faced front. He and Murphy crowded in beside her, the scent of lilac teasing his nose.

When they reached the lobby and stepped outside, the bright sunlight was blinding. Nate pulled on his sunglasses and tightened Murphy's leash.

"Look! Another doggy!" Lucy was gazing around as if she hadn't spent much time out in the general public. Remembering the disastrous state of the Emery household made him scowl. Was it possible Lucy had lived her entire life either inside the squalor of the place or outside in the littered yard?

He fought back a flash of temper, reminding himself that Lucy would be fine now that she was with Willow.

And watching the two of them together was just more proof that he couldn't afford to let his defenses down. Being a part of a family wasn't his thing. He didn't want that, and worse, didn't trust himself to have it.

He had no idea how to be a good husband and father. It was too late for him, but not for Willow and Lucy. When the time was right, they'd find someone to complete their little family.

"Can we have a hot dog, Aunt Willow?" Lucy's head was moving back and forth as she took in the sights and smells of Brooklyn from her stroller.

"Are you hungry already?" Willow's brow furrowed in concern. "We just finished breakfast two hours ago."

Lucy bobbed her head up and down. "I wanna hot dog!"

He quickly intervened. "How about we get a hot dog when it's lunchtime?" When Willow frowned, he added, "My treat."

"Okay." Lucy was satisfied with his response, but Willow couldn't help thinking like a parent.

She leaned in to whisper, "She's been through a lot. But we shouldn't give her everything she wants."

"Oh, sorry." He felt the tips of his ears burn with embarrassment. "I didn't think about that. I just wanted to make her happy. A hot dog seemed like a small price to pay."

Her expression softened. "I know. But part of being a good guardian means setting limits."

We shouldn't give her everything she wants. We? For a moment he lost the ability to think. There was no *we*. There was Willow and Lucy, end of story.

"Nate?"

"Yeah, okay. Got it." He forced the words past his tight throat and changed the subject. "Where is this café of yours anyway?"

"We're going to turn right at the next block. The café should be about halfway down."

Murphy was having a great time. After

they turned the corner, he saw the sign of the Sunshine Sidewalk Café. The sidewalk in front of the restaurant wasn't very wide, but there were four small tables crowded in front of the building. People were sitting outside, enjoying the sixty-degree April weather. Less than a week ago, they'd experienced an unexpected snowstorm, two inches covering the grass and trees, and now it was practically summer. That was spring in New York. Completely unpredictable.

"Would you like a table inside or outside?" A petite woman with short dark hair greeted them.

"Actually, I'm here about the server position." Willow looked nervous. "Have you already filled it?"

"Not yet." The woman thrust out her hand. "I'm Angela Rivera."

"Willow Emery. Are you the manager?"

Angela laughed. "Owner, manager, server, hostess, accountant, you name it."

"It's great to meet you. I'm really interested in the position. As you can see I have a young girl to support. I have a lot of restaurant experience, too."

Nate suddenly heard a panicked shout. "Help! Police! Help!"

What in the world? He turned to look over his shoulder. A young man in a baseball cap and a Yankees jersey was waving his arms in a frantic attempt to get his attention.

"Help! Someone is being attacked!"

He hesitated, unwilling to leave Willow and Lucy there alone. Willow was still chatting with Angela, the two women cooing over Lucy, so he made a split-second decision to respond. "Willow? Stay here. I'll be right back. Come, Murphy."

"This way!" The Yankees fan turned and disappeared around the corner, clearly expecting Nate and Murphy to follow.

Nate broke into a jog, dodging pedestrians while keeping Murphy close to his side. He listened intently but didn't hear any sounds indicating an attack. He hoped he wasn't going to be too late. As they turned the corner, he raked his gaze over the area, searching for anything suspicious.

There was no obvious sign of an attack, but the Yankees fan was still several paces ahead. "Hurry! Over here! In the alley!"

Nate darted around a group of tourists. He came to the spot where the Yankees fan had been, in front of a long narrow alley, but the guy was gone. He'd vanished like some sort of magician's trick.

There was no attack.

His gut clenched with fear. *Willow! Lucy!*

He whirled around and instantly ran back to the café. The sidewalk seemed to stretch forever. He'd followed the stupid Yankees fan farther than he'd realized.

And it had been nothing but a clever ploy to get him and Murphy out of the way.

No! How could he have been so gullible? He quickened his pace, unable to bear the thought of something happening to Willow and Lucy.

He wheeled around the corner, his heart lodged in his throat. Even more people crowded the sidewalks now.

Lucy was crying, loud screeching sobs. "Aunt Willow! Aunt Willow! Come back!"

A pedestrian got in his way and he nearly plowed the guy over in his haste to reach Willow and Lucy.

"No! Stop!" Willow's voice was muffled. He caught a glimpse of someone dressed in black with a hat pulled low over his forehead dragging her toward a black sedan double-parked a few spots up from the café.

"Stop! Police!" He shouted as loud as he could to be heard above the din. Realizing he might be too late, he reached down and released Murphy's leash. "Get him, Murphy. Get him!"

Murphy took off running. Like a racehorse, he closed the gap between him and Willow faster than Nate ever could.

The man with the hat must have realized the same thing, because he abruptly pushed Willow toward Murphy, then spun and took off running in the opposite direction.

It all happened like a scene unfolding in slow motion. Willow tripped over Murphy. His partner yelped as the two of them tangled together. Then Willow hit the pavement with a *thud*. Lucy was still crying, her stroller several feet away from Willow and Murphy.

"Willow! Are you okay?" He finally caught up to them, crouching down to check Willow and his partner. Murphy had managed to free himself from Willow. He was up on his feet, staring in the direction the intruder had gone.

"Get him," Nate repeated. He didn't like sending his partner off alone, but he couldn't leave Willow and Lucy.

The yellow Lab took off, trotting fast, his nose periodically going to the ground.

Murphy could track just about anything, but he wasn't trained to go into subway stations without Nate. A fact he hoped the assailant didn't know, as there was a subway entrance at the opposite end of the block.

"What happened?" He helped Willow to her feet.

"He—came out of nowhere." Her voice was shaky, her hands trembling. Her palms were scraped and bleeding, but she didn't seem to care. "I didn't notice until he grabbed me."

"Shh, it's okay." He caught her in his arms for a quick hug, then turned toward Lucy. Some instinct had him lifting the girl from her stroller and handing her over to Willow. They clung to each other, much the way they had outside the scene of the Emery murders.

His gaze fell on the license plate of the black sedan abandoned by the would-be kidnapper. He quickly memorized the plate number, hoping it would be a clue as to who'd attacked Willow.

A sharp dog bark caught his attention. His heart was hammering, and he desperately wanted to go after Murphy. What if the assailant tried to hurt him? Nate took one step forward, then another, but stopped.

He couldn't leave Willow. He had to trust in his partner's training. The K-9 would soon return.

Murphy came running through the crowd of onlookers, returning to Nate's side.

"Murph!" He went down to his knee and

wrapped his arms around his partner. From what he could tell, Murphy wasn't hurt.

Unfortunately, the assailant had gotten away.

SEVEN

Willow clutched Lucy close, unable to stop trembling. Her shoulders were sore from where the guy had roughly grabbed her, trying to force her into the vehicle. Everything had happened so fast. She'd tried to crane her neck to get a better look at his face, but his arms were like steel bands around her. She'd barely caught a glimpse before Nate had shouted, causing him to roughly shove her toward Murphy.

The only reassuring part of the whole incident was that the attacker hadn't bothered to go after Lucy. Her niece was safe, for now. But glancing back at the Sidewalk Sunshine Café, she was sad to understand there was no way she could work there anytime soon.

Maybe never. The owner, Angela Rivera,

had sounded positive, but had needed someone immediately, not in two weeks or longer.

"Are you okay?" Angela had come over to check on her. "What happened?"

"It's nothing." She tried to smile. "A misunderstanding."

"Are you sure?" Angela's doubt was clearly reflected in her gaze. "When I came out of the kitchen, it looked like that guy was trying to force you into his car."

"I'm safe now, and so is Lucy. Thanks for coming to check on us."

"Sure." Angela gave her one last look, as if sensing Willow was downplaying the event, then hurried back to her customers. For a moment Willow envied her ability to run her own little café, with no worries other than offering good food.

"Run this license plate for me." Nate was kneeling beside Murphy, speaking into the radio on his collar. It took a moment for her to realize he was reciting the plate number belonging to the black sedan. When finished, Nate rose to his feet and turned toward her. “We need to get you and Lucy away from here.”

Rattled by the near miss, she could only nod.

Nate spoke into his cell phone. “Eden? Sorry, I also need you to check video footage from the Bay Ridge Avenue subway station. Perp dressed in black with a black cap pulled over his forehead left less than five minutes ago. I need Belle Montera to call me, ASAP.”

She shivered again and glanced over her shoulder. Pedestrians had originally stopped to gawk at the commotion but were now moving on with their busy lives. It struck her then, her life may not return to normal anytime soon.

No matter how much she wanted it to.

Nate’s phone rang, and he stayed close to her side as he answered. “Belle, thanks for calling me back. I need you and your K-9 to keep a lookout for a man dressed in black with a hat pulled down over his forehead. He just disappeared through the Bay Ridge Avenue station.” There was a pause before he added, "I know it's not much, but do your best, okay? Get Max to help, too. I'm working with Eden to get a photo and I'll shoot it your way as soon as I get it."

It bothered her to know the guy who'd tried to abduct her had gotten away. She sent up a quick prayer, thanking God for sending Nate back in the nick of time to save her.

"I think I've covered all bases for now." Nate slipped his phone back into his pocket.

"Thanks, Nate." She managed a smile over Lucy's head. "Your timing was perfect. If not for you and Murphy, he may have gotten away with me."

He scowled. "Don't thank me, Willow. This is all my fault. I shouldn't have left you in the first place. I should have realized that the fake cry for help was nothing more than a ploy to get you alone."

"Really?" She tilted her head to the side, regarding him thoughtfully. "How could you possibly know that?"

He stared at her for a moment, then looked away. "I just should have."

"And ignore the possibility an innocent

person was in trouble?" She shook her head. "No way. You never could have stayed here, doing nothing. It's not in your nature, Nate. You're a cop. I'm sure you've responded to other ridiculous calls, too."

He let out a heavy sigh. "Maybe you're right. Still, it burns to know that he almost succeeded."

"But he didn't." Willow didn't want Nate to feel guilty about this when it was her decision to come here about the job in the first place.

"Nate?" The sound of a female voice caused Nate to glance over his shoulder. A pretty female K-9 officer with shoulder-length dark hair was coming toward them, accompanied by a large German shepherd. "No sign of him yet, but I let Max know, too."

"Belle, this is Willow Emery. Willow, K-9 officer Belle Montera and her K-9 partner, Justice."

"It's nice to meet you." Willow smiled but felt like a giraffe towering over the petite woman. There weren't too many men who made her feel less conspicuous, but Nate had several inches on her.

More to like about him. Not that it mattered.

"Thanks, Belle. As soon as I get something from Eden, I'll let you know." Nate moved closer to Willow's side and she was touched by his protective stance. "We'll be at the precinct if you need me."

"Sounds good." Belle turned toward the black sedan. "Did you call for a tow truck? We may be able to get a DNA hit from the interior."

"Not yet, but that's a good idea. Will you take care of it?"

"Of course." Belle grinned. "I can tell you want to get out of here."

Nate didn't disagree. "Thanks again." He turned to Willow. "Come on, my SUV is parked near your apartment building."

She buckled Lucy into her stroller. They'd barely gone a block when his phone pinged. He glanced down at the screen, then turned the device so she could see the image. "Recognize him?"

She cupped her hand over the phone to cut down the glare from the sun. The photo was a bit blurred, showing a man wearing all black, a black cap pulled low over his forehead, rushing into the subway station, his head slightly turned to the side.

A chill rippled over her, lifting the hairs on her arms. "Craggy Face."

"Yeah. I think he was the one who ransacked your place." Nate's expression was grim. He worked the phone, no doubt sending the photo to Belle as she was responsible for patrolling the subway stations. She leaned over with a frown. "Hey, is that my photograph of him that you're sending?"

He nodded and glanced up. "Yes, why? It's the one you sent me."

The clarity wasn't great, but she figured it would work well enough for what he needed. "No reason, glad to have something to help your team find him."

"We will. And I'll start with your former boss, Damon. He was photographed talking to the guy, so he must know who he is. We'll catch him, Willow. I promise."

Nate's tone oozed confidence and she wondered if he was putting on a brave act for her benefit. Having her apartment broken into was one thing; being grabbed by Craggy Face and nearly forced into a vehicle was something very different. The moment she'd felt him grab her flashed in her mind's eye. An overwhelming burst of fear had momentarily paralyzed her.

She made a silent promise not to let that happen again. Next time, she needed to keep her wits about her. To fight, with every ounce of strength she possessed, the instant she felt something was wrong.

Lucy needed her, now more than ever.

"Willow, I want you to know, I'll never leave you and Lucy alone like that again."

"I know." His promise touched her heart. "I guess I shouldn't have asked to go to the café."

Nate unlocked his SUV, then turned toward her. "You can't take the job at the café, Willow. Not until we have this guy in custody."

Her shoulders slumped. "I know."

His clear blue eyes burned into hers, seeing too much. "I can help get you whatever you need, including cash. Just trust me, okay?"

She wouldn't take his money—she'd use her savings—but she did trust him. More than she'd ever trusted anyone else.

Maybe she trusted him a little too much. Once she and Lucy were safe, he'd be assigned another case. Moving on in his career, leaving her to focus on raising Lucy.

She needed to remember that this…closeness between them wasn't real. It was temporary. In her experience, men didn't stick around for long.

Despite how much she liked and admired him, there was no possibility of a future with Nate.

The near abduction still had Nate's pulse in the triple digits. And he feared it wouldn't return to normal anytime soon. He hated knowing Willow was in danger.

Nate forced himself to keep his hands at his sides, when all he wanted to do was draw Willow into his arms, holding her and Lucy close.

Why this sudden attachment to a woman he was assigned to protect? He'd never mixed his professional role as cop with his personal life before.

No reason to start now. Yet as he watched Willow buckle Lucy into her car seat, he couldn't help but notice how amazing they were together.

He shook off the unusually tender feelings, forcing himself to concentrate on finding and arresting Craggy Face. He and Murphy had to find him, and soon.

Before he tried again.

When Willow finished with Lucy, she opened the passenger door and slid inside. He put Murphy in the back, then went around to the driver's side, still thinking about their next move. Interviewing Lucy and Willow again wouldn't likely give them too much more to go on, yet it was important to try. He itched to start searching for the owner of the black sedan, but hadn't heard from Eden yet.

He'd been right about the fact that whatever was going on with Willow wasn't connected to the Emery murders. He pulled into traffic, mentally reviewing the similarities between the cold case and this one. Same MO, but what about motive? What did the Emerys have in common with the McGregors?

Other than both sets of victims being Brooklyn residents and lousy parents neglecting their children, what else connected them?

The date. The Emerys were killed on the twentieth anniversary of the McGregors' murders.

But why? What was the missing link? Why had the killer struck again all these years later? Why single out the Emerys as potential victims?

Again, lots of questions and no answers. Yet.

Once Willow and Lucy were safely at the police station, he'd head to the Burgerteria to interview Damon about Craggy Face. But for now, that conversation would have to wait. There was no way the guy who'd just tried to abduct Willow would be hanging around the restaurant with its connection to her. Still, maybe Nate would get something out of the Burgerteria's manager to go on.

The drive to headquarters didn't take long. There was one parking spot left, so he quickly pulled in. His phone rang, and he was relieved to see the K-9 unit's tech guru's name on the screen. "Eden, please tell me you have something on the car."

"It was reported stolen earlier this morning."

He sighed and glanced at Willow. "That figures. Where was it taken from?"

"That's the interesting part. It was stolen from a driveway in Windsor Terrace at zero three hundred hours. The guy apparently came home late, leaving his car in the driveway. He didn't realize the vehicle was missing for several hours."

"How does that help us?"

"It's a crime of opportunity. I'm doing a search on other similar stolen car cases now, to see if I can find a pattern. This may not be the first time these guys have used a stolen car to do their dirty work."

The idea of a connection brought a flash of hope. "That's good stuff, Eden. Thanks."

"I aim to please, Slater." Her airy response made him smile.

He slid the phone back into his pocket and glanced at Willow. "Ready?"

She nodded, but her light brown eyes were clouded with apprehension. Not for her, he knew, but for Lucy. "Sounds like you have a lead."

"We do." He couldn't share all the details of their investigation but wanted to reassure her. "Our K-9 unit is a great team. We'll get this guy soon."

"I'm sure you will. I'll keep praying for God's strength and guidance. I know God is looking out for us."

He was humbled by her faith and wondered once again if he was missing out on something special. Gavin was a believer, as were several other members of the team.

The painful memory of his father screaming curses and smashing his fist into his mother brought him back to reality. He was happy for Willow, but that kind of thing wasn't for him. He and his mother had barely escaped with their lives, and he didn't see how God had anything to do with that.

He took care of Murphy as Willow strapped Lucy into the stroller. Willow glanced at the building in awe, and he understood how she felt. Their new Brooklyn K-9 Unit was housed in an attractive three-story limestone building that had been used as a police precinct many years ago, until that department had merged with another one, moving into a much larger building. It was perfect for their smaller unit and even had diagonal parking along the front of the building, a rarity in New York. A K-9 center was adjacent to the building, housing impressive indoor and outdoor training facilities.

It was an honor to be here, working for Gavin Sutherland and the rest of the team. Nate liked being a K-9 cop. He'd come a long way from the scared kid who'd escaped with his mother from his abusive father all those years ago.

His gaze rested on Willow, her tall, lean frame bent over Lucy. She straightened, her eyes clashing with his. Awareness shimmered between them, so powerful he almost put out a hand to push it away.

"Looks like a nice place to work." Willow's comment cut through the tension.

"Yeah." He took Murphy off the leash, tucking it in his pocket before heading over to join her on the sidewalk. "I'll carry the stroller inside."

She stepped back, giving him room to maneuver. There were three concrete steps leading inside and he easily carried the stroller up and into the building with Murphy on his heels.

Penelope McGregor was working the front desk when they entered. Nate kept his expression neutral, but his heart went out to Penny. The whole unit knew she had to be thinking of her parents' *unsolved* murders. Penny—and her brother—had to be reeling from the news. Especially because, once again, there was very little evidence. And no leads on the killer.

Penny's eyes widened in surprise when she saw them. She quickly jumped out of her seat and came around to meet them, immediately holding her hand out to Willow. "Hi! I'm Penny McGregor. You must be Willow Emery."

"Yes, and this is Lucy." Willow smiled at her niece.

Penny's expression softened as she crouched down beside the little girl. "Hi, Lucy, how are you?"

Lucy didn't seem intimidated by meeting so many strangers, but didn't exactly answer Penny, either. "Doggy." She buried her tiny fingers in Murphy's pale yellow fur. "Nice doggy."

"Yes, Murphy is a good dog." Penny's brown eyes were concerned when they met his. "Might be best to take Lucy into one of the interview rooms. She probably needs some time to relax before we begin."

"Agreed." Penny wasn't a cop, but considering she was the sole witness of her parents' murders, including seeing the perp who'd worn black and a clown face with blue hair, and had also been given the stuffed monkey, he thought it might be a good idea for her to gently question Lucy. "Room A appears to be open. Why don't you get her settled in there?" Willow looked as if she might argue, but he sent a reassuring smile. "It's okay. Penny is good with kids."

"All right." Willow rubbed her hands up and down her arms. "Thanks."

He watched them disappear into the interview room, then took Murphy back past the coffee station to the cubicle area. He crossed over to his desk and booted up his computer, hoping to find Craggy Face's photo in their mug shot files.

Gavin Sutherland poked his head around the edge of his cubicle. "Hey, I heard what happened."

"Yeah." He turned to face his boss, a tall man in his early thirties with dark hair and eyes. Gavin could intimidate the best of them, but the guy had a huge heart. "I don't think this thing going on with Willow

Emery is linked to her brother's and sister-in-law's murders, though."

"It doesn't seem likely, since the MO mirrors the McGregor case and the incidents involving Willow are all connected to those photos the perp stole." Gavin frowned. "You might want to keep *two* eyes on her."

"I plan to. Anything new on Liberty?"

"No, and it's bugging me. That highly skilled Lab is cross-trained in all specialties and we could really use her services."

"I know. She's tops and we need her out there. Instead, a criminal is keeping her from being able to do what she does best: find smuggled contraband." Nate glanced down at Murphy, stretched out at his feet. A flash of anger burned deep in his belly. He wasn't sure what he'd do if someone had put a bounty on his partner's head—and Liberty was one of Murphy's littermates. "Let me know if you need me to do something more."

Gavin touched his shoulder. "I will, Slater. Thanks."

Nate was still thinking of the bounty on

Liberty's head when his phone rang. He quickly answered, hoping for good news. "Slater."

"Nate? It's Belle. With Eden's help we tracked down the subway stop where the perp who tried to abduct Willow exited the train."

"Great." He surged to his feet.

"Hang on," she cautioned. "The guy immediately slid into a car—the driver was obviously waiting for him—and disappeared."

"Disappeared? Did Eden get a plate number?" He tightened his grip on the phone, holding his breath. Eden Chang was their tech guru and if anyone could get something from nothing, she could. At just twenty-seven, she was a master at searching through police and public databases, cross-referencing, and homing in on helpful information.

"No. Unfortunately the plate was obscured with mud and the camera angle was bad. She's playing with the video some more, but so far doesn't have a single letter or digit to use as a possible reference point."

"You've got to be kidding me." He jammed his fingers through his hair, battling a wave of frustration. "So you're telling me this is nothing more than another dead end."

"I'm afraid so." Belle's tone held regret. "Still, we might get some DNA from the car that Craggy Face used in his attempt to kidnap Willow. I have the forensic team working on that right now."

"Thanks." Nate tossed his phone on his desk. First Eden had been unable to trace the cash-paid gas receipt found in Willow's apartment, and now this.

Willow had nearly been kidnapped right in front of his eyes, and he'd have absolutely nothing to go on unless he could get Willow's ex-boss, Damon Berk, to talk.

Not likely, but he'd do his best to make that happen.

EIGHT

Lucy didn't seem too intimidated to be seated beside Penny McGregor, maybe because Penny had started off asking questions about her favorite things, like colors and TV shows.

"You're a very brave girl." Penny placed her arm around Lucy's shoulders, radiating compassion. "And I want you to know you're safe with your aunt Willow."

Lucy nodded, taking a sip from the container of chocolate milk that Penny had given her. Her niece obviously preferred chocolate milk over plain, and Willow made a mental note to stop and pick some up on their way home.

"Lucy, can you tell me again about the bad clown you saw yesterday?" Penny's gaze was kindly sympathetic.

The little girl tensed and shook her head. "Too scary."

"I know, but remember how brave you were to talk to Detective Nate?" Penny gently reminded her. "Can you tell me what happened?"

Willow didn't like the look of distress on Lucy's face. "Maybe it's too soon."

Penny nodded and turned her attention back to Lucy. "I was scared by a mean clown, too, when I was your age."

Lucy's eyes widened. "You were?"

Penny nodded. "A scary, mean clown hurt my mommy and daddy, too. If you can tell me what happened, it will help the police find him and throw him in jail where he belongs."

Lucy glanced at Willow, then back to Penny. "Okay."

"Where were you when he came?"

"I was playing outside when he came into the yard." Lucy's voice had dropped so low it was difficult for Willow to hear her.

Penny nodded encouragingly. "Then what happened?"

"He gave me a bag with a stuffed monkey and told me to stay outside." Lucy's eyes welled with tears. "I don't like monkeys anymore."

"I know. I don't like them, either." Penny gave the little girl another hug. "What did he look like?"

"Blue hair like my dolly."

"Anything else?" Penny gently prodded. "Do you remember what color his eyes were?"

Lucy scrunched up her forehead. "Bad clown with mean eyes."

"Did you stay outside like he told you?"

Lucy nodded, then shook her head. "I heared loud noises. *Bang! Bang!* So I went inside."

Willow wanted to stop her niece there, unwilling to have her relive the moment Lucy hadn't been able to wake up her mommy and daddy, but Penny went on.

"What did you see?"

Lucy's eyes welled with tears. "Mommy and Daddy were on the floor. They wouldn't wake up when I shaked them."

"Okay, that's good, Lucy. You're so brave." Penny stroked her hand over Lucy's wavy hair.

Lucy looked at Willow and Willow's heart squeezed painfully in her chest. "I love you, Lucy."

"I love you, too." Lucy sniffed and swiped at her face.

"Would you like more chocolate milk?" Penny asked.

"Yes." Momentarily distracted by what appeared to be her new favorite drink, Lucy took the carton of milk and sucked what was left through the straw, making a loud noise as she drained every drop from the container.

"I'll be right back." Penny squeezed Lucy's hand, then left the interview room to get the promised chocolate milk.

"We'll go home soon, Lucy, okay?" Willow smiled reassuringly. "Thanks for being so brave."

"Will Murphy stay with us again?"

Uh-oh, the little girl was becoming too attached to Murphy. "We'll see." She couldn't deny she wanted Nate and Murphy there but wasn't sure if Nate's plan to stay had changed.

And she refused to make promises she couldn't keep.

When Penny returned, she brought Nate with her. "Willow, Nate would like you to look at a few photographs if you have a minute."

"Oh, um, now?" She didn't hide her lack of enthusiasm. The last thing she wanted was to keep Lucy here at the precinct longer than necessary.

"It won't take long," Nate assured her. "And it may help us catch the guy who tried to grab you."

"All right." She stood, then bent to press a kiss to the top of Lucy's head. "I'll be back soon, okay?"

"Okay." Lucy didn't seem to mind, her attention centered on Penny as the desk clerk opened another container of chocolate milk.

Nate stood, holding the door open for her, with Murphy standing patiently at his side. She followed him past a coffee stand, taking note of the large map of Brooklyn hanging on the wall, until they reached his work station. Murphy dropped down beside the desk, as if he were used to this.

"We have computer-generated mug shots." Nate gestured to his chair. "Have a seat. I entered the hard copy and facial features that match your Craggy Face guy into the database."

She took his chair, keenly aware of his woodsy scent as he leaned over her shoulder to work the mouse. This ridiculous awareness of him had to stop. She was sure he wasn't interested in her and even if he was, she had to focus on adopting and raising her orphaned niece and finding a job that would still allow her a lot of time with Lucy.

"There are six images on a page," Nate was saying. "Could be that Craggy Face was picked up for a crime at some point when he was younger. You have a good eye—let me know if any of these guys look familiar."

His offhand compliment shouldn't have made her feel good, but it did. She turned her attention to the screen, rejecting the first page of images, then the second. She tried not to rush through them, but as she clicked through page after page, she knew in her gut that Craggy Face wasn't any of these men, now or when he was younger.

"I'm sorry, Nate." She sat back in the chair with a sigh, turning to glance up at him. "I don't think he's in your system."

"Yeah, I'm getting that impression, as well." He had to be as frustrated as she was, but he didn't show it. His phone rang and he reached around her to snag the receiver. "Slater."

There was a pause as he listened to whoever was on the other end of the line. She clicked through a few more images for something to do but couldn't help but listen to his side of the conversation. He was clearly talking to someone who'd been working on a lead.

"Thanks, Darcy. I appreciate you letting me know."

"No prints on the black sedan?" It was a logical assumption.

"Darcy's still working on evidence from your brother's house, but she asked another tech to put a rush on the black sedan for me. No match in the system." He shrugged. "At least there's a print. Could belong to the owner, too. They have someone heading out to get his prints to compare against now."

She didn't understand why he looked so dejected. "But a fingerprint is a good thing, right?" She thought back to those terrifying moments when she struggled with Craggy Face, then frowned. "No, it's not a good thing. I'm pretty sure he was wearing gloves."

"When he grabbed you?" When she nodded, Nate sighed again. "Well, it's possible he wasn't wearing gloves when he stole the vehicle. Or maybe Craggy Face had someone stealing the car for him, and that guy didn't wear gloves. Criminals aren't always as smart as they think they are."

She liked how he turned a negative into a potential positive. "Let's hope the print leads to something good." She rose from his desk chair. "Is it okay if I take Lucy home now?"

"Would you mind hanging out here for a while longer?" He walked beside her as they made their way back to the interview rooms. "I need to take Murphy back to the Burgerteria to question Damon Berk, your former boss. It shouldn't take me too long."

She didn't like the idea of staying in the police station, but it was probably better to wait for Nate to take her and Lucy home. "I guess, but it's a nice day out and it would be good for Lucy to play outside. I'm worried she'll get bored sitting around in my apartment."

Nate nodded. "I get it." He opened the door to the interview room. "Penny? I'd like to take Willow and Lucy on a quick tour of the station, introduce them to the crew, and I'm wondering if you'd mind arranging for Willow and Lucy to have a tour of the K-9 training center afterward?"

"Of course." Penny grinned at Lucy. "Would you like to see more doggies?"

"Yes!" Lucy jumped off her seat. "I love doggies."

Willow reluctantly smiled. "Sounds like fun."

Nate nodded. "Our tour begins, then," he

said, gallantly sweeping his hand forward. "Follow me, ladies."

Lucy giggled, and Willow and the little girl trailed behind Nate around the front of the main desk where Penny had been sitting when they'd arrived.

"This is everyone's first stop," Nate said. "Need to talk to an officer, report a crime, offer a tip? You speak to Penny McGregor. She's very important to the team."

Lucy's eyes widened with admiration at Penny, who'd returned to her seat.

"And behind Penny's desk is where all the police work happens," Nate added.

Willow took in the many desks, officers hunched over computers and phones, typing, taking notes, talking, comparing information, dashing from one desk to another and to the back offices. And a lot of sipping from take-out coffee cups. The big room was hopping with activity. Last night, Nate had told her about his unit and his colleagues, and it was clear from the warm way he'd described them, sharing a bit about why each had become a cop, that they were already close, despite being a new unit operating for only a few months. As she glanced around the big room, she recognized some of the team based on his descriptions.

Tall, lanky Raymond Morrow, a narcotics K-9 officer who'd been poring over reports for evidence in a drug case he was working on, stood up and came around his desk. He smiled at Willow, then knelt in front of Lucy and extended his hand. "You must be Lucy. It's very nice to meet you. I'm Ray. My partner, a furry springer spaniel named Abby, is in the kennel right now, but she'd love to meet you when you head over."

"I'd like that," Lucy said shyly.

Willow watched Nate send Ray an appreciative nod. Nate had mentioned he didn't know too much about Raymond's past, but he knew the dedicated officer had a difficult family background related to why he became a narcotics cop. His kindness to Lucy was touching.

Next they ran into bomb detection K-9 officer Henry Roarke, who at six foot four towered over Lucy to the point that she had to tip her head way back. Henry was African American and wore his curly black hair military short, but despite his height, he laughed and knelt down, too. He told Lucy a cute knock-knock joke and Lucy giggled. A warm, funny guy, Henry seemed a natural around kids, probably due to having raised his teenage sister after the loss of their parents. Willow was surprised she could remember so much about what Nate had shared.

Nate glanced around and reminded her she'd already met K-9 transit officer Belle Montera and her German shepherd partner, Justice. Willow recognized officer Vivienne Armstrong, with her short dark hair, on the phone at her desk and taking furious notes.

Willow couldn't recall what Nate had told her about the tall, dark-haired, green-eyed officer walking toward them. He introduced himself as Jackson Davison, who also worked in Emergency Services, and shared a cute story about his chocolate Lab partner, Smokey.

"Hi, Lucy!" said blond K-9 detective Tyler

Walker once he got off the phone. He spun around his desk chair. "Want to see a photo of my partner, Dusty? She's a golden retriever and a great finder." Willow remembered Nate mentioning that Tyler was the single parent of a toddler daughter.

"I'm good at hide-and-seek, too," Lucy said, her shyness evaporating.

Tyler grinned, and his phone rang, so he grabbed it.

Nate glanced around again, and Willow had the feeling he was looking for K-9 detective Bradley McGregor, Penny's brother. From what Nate had shared, Bradley had been through so much as a teen when he and Penny's parents were killed. Willow didn't see anyone matching his description. Bradley must be out on a case.

Penny stood up and let them know the training center next door was all set for Willow and Lucy's tour.

Nate thanked Penny, then turned to Willow. "I'll be back as soon as possible." He lightly squeezed her shoulder before turning away. "Come, Murphy."

Willow watched as Nate left the precinct with Murphy. She found it hard to believe Damon had anything to do with ransacking her home, but the man *had* been photographed with the guy who'd tried to wrestle her into the black car. Maybe Damon had nothing to do with it, and Craggy Face had simply noticed her taking pictures, realized she must have gotten one of him and panicked. Why, she had no idea. Hopefully Nate would get some information about the guy out of Damon. He wasn't the nicest person but he'd always been reasonably fair.

This weird loneliness she felt watching Nate go had to be related to the danger surrounding her.

It was nothing personal. She knew from past experience with men, including her father, who'd walked out when she was only two years old, that once Nate had Craggy Face in custody, she wouldn't see him again.

Nate couldn't believe how difficult it was to walk away from Willow, feeling her gaze on his back. It was strange how close they'd gotten in such a short period of time. Even from this distance, he could pick up the lilac scent of her.

Or maybe it was all in his head.

He shook off the strange and unwelcome sensation and focused on what was important. He couldn't afford to get emotionally involved with Willow or her adorable niece. She and Lucy deserved to be safe, and that meant he needed to remain professional. Getting emotionally involved increased the chance of making a mistake. He needed to focus on the two cases. The Emery murders and the attempted abduction of Willow.

He knew better than to hope for success on the fingerprint found on the sedan, but he'd try to get a name out of Damon Berk, the manager of the Burgerteria.

Outside, he glanced up, taking note of clouds gathering overhead. Spring could be dicey, the temperature rising like the sun, then falling like a rock. He quickened his pace, knowing that a rainstorm could easily wash away any remaining scent left behind by Craggy Face.

"Up, Murphy." He lifted the back hatch for his partner. Murphy jumped gracefully inside the crated area.

The drive to the Burgerteria didn't take nearly as long as it took to find a parking spot. He would have walked, if not for the impending storm. When he found a spot, he let Murphy out.

They were still fifty yards from the restaurant, which was fine with him. He once again opened the evidence bag containing the gas receipt. "Seek, Murphy. Seek!"

It only took Murphy a moment to pick up the scent. His partner followed the same path he had the evening before, the scent trail leading to the doorway of the restaurant where Willow once worked.

"Good boy." He leaned down to give Murphy a brisk rub. Then he opened the door to the restaurant. "Seek!"

Murphy eagerly complied, nose to the ground as he crossed the threshold.

"Hey! We don't allow dogs in here!"

Nate glanced up from Murphy to find Damon Berk scowling at him from across the room. He held up his badge. “Police business.”

“Wh-what?” Damon sputtered. “It doesn’t matter if you’re a cop. I run a restaurant. Having an animal in here violates all kinds of health codes.”

Nate ignored Damon’s mini rant, his gaze centered on Murphy. His partner had followed the scent to a vacant table near the door and sat, waiting expectantly for his praise.

“Good boy, Murph.” He again rubbed the animal’s silky coat. This time, he walked the animal farther inside the restaurant. “Seek, Murphy.”

Murphy put his nose to the ground, sniffing around the area. They were garnering attention from the other customers, but Nate didn’t care. Despite his attempt to widen the search area, Murphy eventually ended up back at the entrance to the restaurant. Within minutes, his partner quickly returned to the same spot as before, sitting right in front of a high-top table with two seats.

“Good boy.” He gave Murphy a final pat,

then straightened. He caught the manager's attention by raising his voice. "Damon Berk? I have a few questions for you. We can talk here or outside, your choice."

"What is this about?" Damon was clearly put off by his arrival. "I have a business to run."

"This shouldn't take too long." Nate gestured to the vacant high-top table. "Here? Or outside?"

Berk glanced over his shoulder, taking note of how many of his customers were watching them with frank curiosity. "Outside."

"Fine with me." Nate opened the door and waited for Berk to pass through first. He followed with Murphy at his side. "Heel."

Murphy sat.

Damon Berk didn't seem impressed. "What do you want?"

Nate raised a brow at his curt tone. "My name is Detective Slater and I have a few questions. What is your role here and how long have you been employed?"

"I'm the manager and have been since we opened."

"And when was that?"

"Three years ago." Despite how the air had cooled beneath the gathering storm clouds, Nate noticed a bead of sweat forming at Berk's temple.

"Is that how long Willow Emery was working here before you fired her?"

Damon blanched. "Yes. Is that what this is about? Listen, I didn't fire her, she quit."

Nate wanted to badger him more about that, but decided it was better to get to the point about Craggy Face. "Okay, now I'd like to ask about one of your customers." He pulled out his phone and tapped on the screen, bringing up the photo Willow had taken of Craggy Face. "I need to know this man's name."

Damon barely looked at the screen. "I don't know him."

"Really?" Nate glanced at the photo again, then captured Damon's gaze. "Because you're talking to him here in what appears to be more than a casual conversation. Take a closer look."

Damon shifted his feet nervously, a bead of sweat rolling slowly down the side of his face. But he obeyed Nate's request, leaning over to peer intently at the screen. Damon's brow was furrowed with what was supposed to look like concentration. Nate wasn't buying it; he felt sure the manager knew the guy who'd tried to abduct Willow, but wasn't surprised when he once again repeated, "Sorry. I don't know him."

"You don't remember what you were discussing with him?"

Damon's gaze darted right and left, as if fearing they were being watched. "I talk to a lot of my customers, but it doesn't mean anything. Schmoozing is part of the hospitality business. I'm always hoping they return to the restaurant again—that's part of keeping this place afloat. But I don't ask their names or get any other personal information from them. That would be crossing the line."

"Funny, but this doesn't look like schmoozing to me." Nate tapped his index finger on the phone screen. "Looks like an intense conversation, maybe even an argument."

Another bead of sweat rolled down Damon's face. "Maybe he was upset by the food. I often reassure customers that if they don't like their meal I'll give them a discount to return." Berk brightened. "Yes, now I remember! This man requested to speak to me about a problem with his burger. He'd cracked his tooth on something hard inside the beef and was demanding I do something about it."

"Did you pay for his tooth?" Nate planned to ask for proof of payment, even though he didn't really believe him.

"I—uh, well, no." Damon didn't fall for his trap. "I didn't charge him for his meal and told him he could return anytime for a free lunch or dinner on me."

"And you didn't get his name?"

Berk spread his hands wide. "Why would I? I wasn't even sure he'd take me up on my offer. He was pretty upset about his tooth."

"Right. When was this broken tooth incident, exactly?"

Damon waved a hand. "I don't know, not recently."

"That's interesting, because Murphy picked up his scent at the high-top table near the door." He wasn't about to let Berk know that Willow's photo was stamped with a date and time.

Damon paled, then backpedaled. "Well, it could have been the past week or so, I didn't exactly take the time to write the complaint down on my calendar. Now if you'll excuse me, I have a lot of work to do. With Willow gone, I have a trainee in the kitchen."

"Just one more question," Nate said. "Where were you on Sunday evening?"

"Here at the restaurant, then at home." Another bead of sweat rolled down his face. "Why? Are you accusing me of something?"

"Just curious. But I do need something else from you."

Berk looked impatient. "Now what?"

"If this man shows up again, I'd like you to call me." Nate fished out a business card and held it out for him. Damon stared at it as if it might bite him before he reluctantly took it.

"Fine. But I doubt he'll be back anytime soon. It's not like he's one of my regular customers."

"Still, I'd appreciate a call when he does return."

Damon shoved the card into his pocket, then hurried back inside the restaurant. Nate watched through the window as Berk quickly wove his way toward the back of the restaurant.

To check on his trainee cook? No, he felt certain Damon had gone straight back to call Craggy Face. Too bad he didn't have enough evidence to request a search warrant for Berk's phone records. The photo alone wasn't enough; Berk claimed he was a disgruntled customer, and he didn't have any way to dispute his claim.

Nate wasn't sure what business the two of them had together, but sensed it was illegal.

Why else were they so desperate to get their hands on Willow's photograph?

NINE

The K-9 training center was an impressive facility, but Willow couldn't help glancing at her watch every few minutes, wondering when Nate would return.

This strange attachment she was feeling toward him bothered her. She and Lucy were safer here, surrounded by two-legged and four-legged cops, than anywhere else.

Still, she felt oddly vulnerable without him. Which wasn't good. She really needed to find a way to put distance between them.

At least Lucy was enjoying herself. Penny had given them a tour of the kennels and the indoor training yard, and now they were in the outdoor yard, which was fully fenced in. The little girl had managed to shake off the effects of the interview and had run through the K-9 obstacle course pretending to be Murphy.

"I'm a doggy, woof woof!" Lucy went down on her hands and knees and crawled through a colorful flexible tunnel.

She couldn't help but smile at her niece's antics. The little girl displayed an incredible imagination and she couldn't help wondering if that was related to how much time Lucy spent alone without parental supervision. Just remembering how Lucy had been outside by herself when the killer had approached was horrifying.

Her smile faded as the reality of her situation hit hard, stealing her breath. When exactly would the woman from Child Protective Services, Jayne Hendricks, show up for a surprise visit? What if Ms. Hendricks learned about her close call with Craggy Face? Would she decide that leaving Lucy in Willow's care would be too dangerous? Would she demand the little girl be placed into foster care until the threat against Willow was gone?

As much as she couldn't bear the idea of

Lucy being in danger, she felt strongly her niece needed to be with someone familiar, not a houseful of strangers.

She closed her eyes for a moment, silently praying that God would continue to look over them, keeping them safe in His care, and allow Lucy to remain in her custody.

"Lucy, sweetie, that hurdle is only for furry friends, not humans."

Penny's voice caught her attention. She glanced over to see Lucy reaching up to grab on to a small hurdle that was used for the dogs to jump over. Willow pulled herself together and hurried to her niece, sweeping Lucy into her arms, trying to make a game out of it.

"I've got you!" She twirled in a circle before setting Lucy back on her feet. "We have to be careful, Lucy, these are set up for the doggies, not for kids to play on."

"I'm a doggy, woof!"

She stifled a sigh, startling when her phone rang. When she pulled the device from the pocket of her pink hoodie, her heart gave a betraying thump when she recognized Nate's number.

"Hello?"

"Hi, Willow, I just wanted to let you know Murphy and I are on the way back to the precinct. How are things going?"

"We're fine. Lucy is pretending to be a dog. Can't you hear her barking?"

"Woof! Woof!" Lucy shouted.

Nate's low chuckle sent shivers of awareness down her spine. "Cute. I should be there in ten minutes, maybe less depending on traffic. I thought we might want to make good on our promise to have hot dogs for lunch."

"Fine with me. Thanks."

"See you soon." Nate disconnected from the call.

Penny crossed over to stand next to Willow and gave her an assuring smile. "Well, Lucy," she called, "it's time to go back to the station. I hope you can come visit the doggies again."

"I hope so, too!" Lucy said with a grin, taking one last look around at her new furry friends as she crawled over on her hands and knees, still in her doggy persona. Willow smiled and decided to let her continue at least until they were outside the building.

Penny led the way and when they reached the concrete sidewalk, Lucy must have decided the cement hurt her knees because she scrambled to her feet. "Aunt Willow, I'm hungry."

"I know. Don't worry, Detective Nate will be here soon. Do you remember what he promised you could have for lunch?"

Lucy scrunched up her face, thinking. "Hot dogs?"

"That's right. We're having hot dogs for lunch."

Penny glanced at her with a warm smile. "Sweet of Nate to take you and Lucy out for lunch."

Willow felt her cheeks burn and quickly shook her head. "It's nothing, really. He's just being nice while protecting us."

"Hmm." Penny's knowing expression indicated otherwise, but Willow sensed arguing further would only reinforce her beliefs. Better not to bring that on.

Back inside the precinct, Penny gestured toward the interview room they'd used earlier. "Why don't you and Lucy wait in there? Your stroller is still inside, too." She knelt down in front of Lucy. "Thanks for talking to me today, Lucy. I had fun showing you the dogs."

Lucy grinned and said, "Me, too," and Penny returned to her seat behind the front desk. The officer who'd taken over in her absence left with a smile at the three of them.

"Sounds good. And thanks for the tour. It was nice that you let Lucy play outside for a while." Willow was truly grateful for Penny's assistance with Lucy.

"It's the least I could do." Penny's gaze dropped to Lucy, who was occupied a few feet away by the basket of toys and stuffed animals Nate had told her the unit kept for little visitors "I know only too well what your niece is going through. As you know, I was Lucy's age the night my parents were murdered. My older brother, Bradley, was spending the night at a friend's house. A man dressed in black, wearing a clown mask with blue hair, came in through our backyard, where I was playing. He gave me a stuffed monkey, then went inside the house. I heard the gunshots, but was too little to understand what had happened."

"I'm so sorry." Willow knew that Penny had suffered through a murder that was exactly like Lucy's, but she shivered at the similarities between the two cases.

"I'm grateful that I have my brother. It's nice that Lucy has you, Willow." Penny flashed a sad smile, then quickly picked up the phone when it rang, understandably relieved for a reprieve from the harrowing conversation.

Willow wondered about the terrifying similarities. The same killer was back? Why? Could there be a connection between Penny's parents and Alex and Debra? Something they had in common? Twenty years ago, Willow's brother had been nine years old. It seemed so strange to think that the same killer had targeted Alex and his wife all these years later.

It didn't make any sense.

Willow ushered Lucy into the interrogation room, and the little girl went straight to a book and doll that Penny must have put on the table before the tour. The door opened, revealing Nate and Murphy. She had to tamp down the urge to greet him with a hug as if he'd been gone for days rather than a couple of hours. "Hey, are you two ready to go?"

"Yes." She rose to her feet and reached for the stroller, searching his gaze. "How was the interview?"

He shrugged. "Berk denied knowing the guy, claimed their conversation was related to an 'anonymous customer' being upset that he'd cracked a tooth on a burger."

"What? No way. I would have remembered something like a chipped tooth. I can't imagine Damon wouldn't have told me about that, considering I make the burgers. He never hesitated to tell me about food complaints."

"I know. I'm pretty sure he wasn't being honest with me."

It bothered her to know that Damon Berk had lied to the police. What sort of shady dealings had her former boss gotten involved in? Something bad enough to send someone to break into her apartment to find the photographs, and to risk attempting to kidnap her right off the street.

"Willow?"

"Yes?" She met his gaze, realizing she'd been lost in her thoughts. "Sorry, what did you say?"

"Are you and Lucy ready to head out?"

She nodded. "Of course. Come on, Lucy, time to get back in the stroller."

She half expected an argument, but Lucy willingly came over. After buckling Lucy into the stroller, she pushed it through the doorway.

"I'll carry her down the stairs." The muscles in Nate's arms bulged as he lifted the stroller and carried it down the few steps leading to the sidewalk. He gestured toward the parking spaces. "I'm at the end of the row."

She pushed Lucy's stroller down the sidewalk. "Where would you like to get our hot dogs? There's a vendor that usually sits a few blocks down from my apartment."

Nate opened the back passenger door, so Willow could place Lucy in her car seat. "I was thinking it might be nice to eat at Owl's Head Park." He glanced up at the overcast sky. "According to my weather app we have a few hours before the rain hits."

"That sounds nice." Willow hoped he didn't notice her pink cheeks. She knew better than to treat this little outing as a date, as she knew full well that Nate was only looking out for her and Lucy's welfare.

"They have hot dog stands around the park, so we'll pick up something there." He took the stroller, folded it up and slipped it on the floor of the back seats. Then he let Murphy in the back. "This helps me, too," he confided, once they were both buckled in. "I need to spend some time playing with Murphy. He worked hard again today."

There, see? Not a date. "He's so smart." Willow glanced over her shoulder, watching as Murphy pressed his nose against the wire crate near Lucy. Even with the barrier between them, she sensed that his intent was to protect the little girl.

Willow settled back in her seat, reminding herself that she needed to be thankful for Nate and Murphy's presence. For their protection and dedication to finding the man who'd killed her brother and his wife, and the guy who'd tried to kidnap her.

It would be selfish and wrong to wish for anything more.

Nate told himself that the main reason he was taking Willow and Lucy to the park was because he needed to reward Murphy. And because he'd promised Lucy a hot dog.

But deep down, he knew that wasn't the entire truth.

No, this little trip to the park was his attempt to make Willow happy.

For being a guy who didn't intend to have a family of his own, he couldn't deny how he'd grown attached to Willow and her niece. He'd laughed upon hearing Lucy barking like a dog and it occurred to him that he hadn't laughed like that in a long time.

He'd always been focused on work, on taking criminals off the streets. His personal life was always secondary, not deemed a priority.

So why was he making Willow and Lucy a priority now?

Sure, his job was to keep them safe, and that might be easier to do while being in her apartment rather than out in the park.

Not that he was really worried about their safety. He trusted Murphy to alert them to any potential danger, especially since he had Craggy Face's scent.

It took a while for him to find a parking spot, but he managed to snag one that wasn't far from the park entrance. He kept a wary eye on the cloudy sky as he followed Willow, who pushed Lucy's stroller along the sidewalk.

Murphy's nose worked as he took in the new scents surrounding them. Willow headed straight for one of the hot dog stands.

"We'll take two hot dogs," Willow said, digging in her purse for her wallet.

"Make it three, my treat." He nudged her aside so he could pay for their meal. "And make mine a chili dog." He turned to Lucy. "What would you like on yours?"

"I just like plain hot dogs!" Lucy said.

Willow smiled. "I'll take mine with mustard and sauerkraut."

"And now what to drink?" Nate asked.

"Chocolate milk!" Lucy said, kicking her heels with excitement.

"Add a chocolate milk, and—" He turned to Willow. "What would you like to drink?"

"Water is fine." She looked nonplussed at his taking over the food ordering.

"Add one root beer and one water," he told the vendor. "Thanks."

"No problem." The woman handed over a cardboard tray loaded with the hot dogs. He passed it to Willow so he could take the drinks.

"You didn't have to pay for our lunch. I'm not destitute." Willow's voice was quiet as they headed toward the closest picnic table.

He pushed the stroller, as Willow's hands were full.

"I never said you were. But this was my idea, remember?" He set the drinks down, then took the hot dogs and napkins from her. "Playing is an important reward for K-9 training, so it really is critical that I spend some time throwing the ball for Murphy."

"I guess I didn't realize it was such a big deal." She released Lucy from the stroller and set her on the bench of the picnic table. She quickly unpacked the food, giving Lucy the milk first, before opening the wrapper around the hot dog.

Willow watched Lucy eat with gusto before taking a tentative bite of her own hot dog. "Delicious."

"Of course. All New York City hot dogs are delicious." Nate grinned as he quickly ate his chili dog. "I may have seconds."

Willow smiled and he was struck again by her beauty. When he'd finished his hot dog, he wiped his hands and took Murphy off his leash.

"Sit." Murphy sat, his gaze going from

Nate's pocket back up to his face. He waited a long moment before reaching in and pulling out the bright orange ball.

Murphy strained forward, his gaze locked on the orange ball.

"Get it!" Nate threw the ball and Murphy took off like a rocket after it, capturing the ball in his mouth and then rushing back to him.

They repeated the sequence several more times, Murphy loping back and forth, ears flopping as he gamely fetched the ball. Lucy came running over.

"Can I throw the ball?"

It wasn't part of the training, but he couldn't stand the idea of disappointing the little girl. "Sure." He crouched beside her, then looked at Murphy. "Sit. Stay."

Murphy sat, tongue lolling, sides heaving from exertion. Still, his gaze didn't waver from the ball.

Lucy threw the ball, but it only went a foot. Murphy cocked his head to the side, as if confused, but then went over to pick up the ball. He dropped it in front of Lucy, then sat.

"I'll help you," Nate offered. He picked up the ball and helped Lucy throw it a little farther this time. Murphy didn't hesitate to chase after it.

"I want to throw it far like you." Lucy gazed up at him with her wide cinnamon eyes.

His heart squeezed and for a moment he imagined what it would be like to be a father to a little girl just like Lucy. Then as quickly as the thought formed, he shoved it away.

"You'll be able to throw it farther when you grow up to be big and strong." Nate picked up the orange ball and stood. He tossed it again for Murphy, watching his partner gallop across the grassy area to fetch it.

A few minutes later, he tucked the ball away and bent to give Murphy a rub. "Good boy, yes, you're such a good boy."

"I have water left, if he needs it." Willow lifted her water bottle toward him.

"It's okay, there's actually water in the

back of my SUV." He glanced at the picnic table; the waste from their meal was cleared away. "Ready to return to your place?"

"Of course. I know you have things to do."

He lifted a brow. "I'm planning to camp out on your sofa again, if you don't mind."

"Oh, um, sure. If you think that's necessary." She looked flustered and he wondered what she was thinking. Had she expected him to drop her and Lucy off and head back to work?

Gavin had given him permission to work from Willow's place, so he could keep an eye on her. But maybe she didn't want him and Murphy invading her personal space.

"Just a couple more nights," he assured her. "I'm sure we'll get this guy soon."

"I know you will. It's truly not a problem." Willow put Lucy in the stroller. "Thanks for the picnic. This was really nice."

The clouds overhead were growing darker and he realized they'd stayed out longer than he'd intended. "We better hurry, or we might get drenched."

He connected Murphy to his leash, then

followed Willow toward the park entrance. The low rumble of thunder reached his ears, so he quickened his pace.

Murphy began to growl low in his throat. Nate glanced at his partner in surprise. Normally Murphy didn't react like this to bad weather.

"What is it, boy?" He glanced around the area, searching for something that may have caught his K-9's attention. There weren't many people in the park, and those who were there were scurrying toward the exits as well in an effort to beat the rain.

More growling, then Murphy abruptly put his nose to the ground. Nate frowned. Was it possible Murphy had picked up Craggy Face's scent?

He reached for the evidence bag. "Seek, Murphy. Seek!"

Murphy took in the scent and quickly alerted along the edge of the sidewalk.

Craggy Face was here? Nate's heart thudded in his chest. "Willow? We need to hurry."

As much as he wanted to keep Murphy on

the scent, he didn't like having Willow and Lucy out in the open. He huddled behind her, protecting her with his body as much as possible as he urged her toward his SUV.

It wasn't far, but the ten feet stretched for what seemed like ten miles. He quickly opened the rear passenger door. Before Willow could get Lucy out of her stroller, a sharp retort echoed through the air.

"Get down!" Nate curled his body over Willow and Lucy, the open door offering some protection from the right. Lucy began to cry, and he could hear Willow softly praying.

He grabbed his radio. "Shots fired at Owl's Head Park! Officer requesting backup. Hurry!"

Murphy continued to growl low in his throat. Nate couldn't move; he needed to protect Willow and Lucy.

He kept himself positioned so that he was a human wall in front of Willow, Lucy and Murphy, braced for the inevitable impact from a bullet.

TEN

Dear Lord, keep us safe in Your care!

Willow repeated the prayer over and over as she clutched Lucy close, reassured by how Nate covered her back. Lucy's tears ripped at Willow's heart and she would have done anything to prevent her niece from reliving the sound of gunfire, a horrifying reminder of her parents' murders. Murphy crowded close, his low growls seeming non-stop.

Craggy Face wouldn't stop until he had her—or the camera with the digital proof of him at the Burgerteria. Why was the photo so important? Because it put him with Damon? Because it placed him in the restaurant? She had no idea and could not figure out what was behind all this. He had to figure that she'd shared the photo with police, so what was the point of coming after her?

She strained to listen, fearing more gunfire, but all she could hear was the roll of thunder, the air thick with humidity.

"Are you okay?" Nate's voice was low and husky near her ear. "You and Lucy weren't hit?"

"No physical injuries." She didn't add that she and Lucy couldn't possibly be all right, now knowing someone had actually aimed a gun and fired at them. But she tried to reassure her niece. "Shh, Lucy, it's okay. Detective Nate and Murphy will keep us safe."

"I want my Mommy." Lucy's wail stabbed deep. It was the one thing Willow couldn't do for the little girl. She couldn't bring back her mommy or her daddy.

"I know, baby, but I'm here. I love you, Lucy. We're going to be okay." Willow wondered if she repeated that often enough, she and Lucy might actually come to believe it.

The faint sound of police sirens grew louder as Nate's backup came rushing to the scene. Willow tentatively lifted her head, her gaze finding the reassuring red-and-blue swirling lights. They'd arrived quickly, but those tense moments had stretched endlessly.

Fat drops of rain splattered against her, and she had the ridiculous hope that the storm may chase away the gunman.

Nate didn't move away from her and Lucy until a member of his team arrived. When he stepped back, a cool breeze made her shiver. Willow lifted Lucy and placed her in the car seat, so she would be protected from the rain. Turning, she recognized dark-haired Vivienne and her K-9, Hank, from the station tour earlier and also the previous day.

Was it really only twenty-four hours ago?

"How many shots were fired?" Vivienne asked.

"Just one, came from the east." Nate's expression was grim. "Murphy picked up the scent just before the gunfire, but I had to get Willow and Lucy out of harm's way. I need to go back and see if Murphy can find it again, before the rain washes the scent away."

"Go. I'll stay here." Vivienne smiled sweetly at Lucy, then gestured to the vehicle. "Willow, you should get inside. I won't let you two out of my sight, promise."

She wasn't going to argue. She decided to sit beside Lucy's car seat in the back, rather than up front. The little girl had stopped crying, but her tear-streaked expression was forlorn. Willow bent close to kiss her forehead.

"Where's Murphy?" Lucy rubbed at her eyes, looking exhausted. Willow wondered if her niece needed a nap.

"He's with Detective Nate. They'll be back soon." At least, she hoped so. Gazing over Lucy's head through the window, she could see Nate and Murphy making their way along the sidewalk not far from where they'd been just a few minutes earlier.

Knowing that Murphy had picked up the scent gave her a flare of hope. Maybe the K-9 would find Craggy Face so Nate could arrest him, putting an end to this nightmare once and for all.

Nate and Murphy headed east, toward a cluster of trees. Her heart thudded painfully as Nate held his weapon ready, clearly expecting the worst.

The inside of the car window grew foggy with their breath, so she reached over to lower the window just enough so she could see. The minutes dragged before Nate and Murphy returned.

"Find something?" Vivienne walked toward him.

"This." Nate held up a plastic evidence bag. She squinted trying to see what was inside, swallowing hard when she caught a glimpse of brass. A bullet? Her stomach knotted, then she realized that wasn't right. It was a shell casing from a bullet. "I'm hoping the forensic team can come up with a match in the system."

"Good work," Vivienne said.

"It was all Murphy." Nate bent and rubbed his K-9, who immediately shook his body to get rid of the rainwater. "We need to spread out in a half circle, see if we can find the bullet."

"Let's go." Ignoring the weather, Vivienne and Hank went one way as Nate and Murphy went the other. More K-9 cops joined them and together they widened their search area, wiping the rain from their eyes as they scoured the ground.

After roughly twenty minutes, they returned to the SUV. Nate scowled. "Nothing."

Vivienne shrugged. "Likely his aim was off."

If that was the case, Willow was thankful for it. She felt blessed. God had truly been watching over them.

Nate brought Murphy toward the car, trailed by the additional K-9 cops. "Willow, this is Officer Max Santelli, his K-9, Sam, and you met Tyler Walker and his K-9, Dusty, earlier today."

She nodded. "Thanks for your help."

"We're a team," Max said with a shrug. "We always have each other's backs."

"I'm going to take Willow and Lucy home." Nate glanced back at them. "I'll follow up with Sarge later."

"Okay. Thanks for the backup, Max and

Ty." Vivienne waved at the two K-9 officers as she and Hank headed for her vehicle.

"Anytime." The taller of the two, Max had dark hair and eyes; his K-9, Sam, was an intimidating-looking rottweiler. Ty Walker's K-9, Dusty, was a pretty golden retriever. She was impressed with how well they all worked together as a team.

Nate opened the back to let Murphy jump in, then came around to slide in behind the wheel.

She glanced at Lucy, relieved to find that the little girl had fallen asleep. All the playing and crying had worn her out to the point that the car doors closing didn't wake her up.

Nate's gaze met hers in the rearview mirror. "I'm sorry." The words were quiet in deference to Lucy's sleeping.

"For what? This wasn't your fault. Thanks to Murphy and your quick thinking, we weren't hurt. God was watching over all of us today."

Nate's self-recriminating expression indicated he felt otherwise. But he didn't say anything more as he pulled away from the curb, his attention now on the rain-washed road in front of him. It troubled her that he didn't lean on God or his faith. Because he hadn't grown up hearing God's word? Or because he'd lost it along the way?

Something never learned could be taught and something lost could be found.

If the will was strong enough.

She wanted, needed to help Nate find his way, to learn to accept God's strength and support.

The pelting rain didn't let up until they neared her apartment. Nate found a parking spot that wasn't too far and pulled in. He glanced back at her. "You want me to carry Lucy?"

She felt physically and emotionally exhausted. "Yes, please."

He nodded, sliding out from behind the wheel. She pushed out of the seat as he let Murphy out, standing back as the dog once again shook off the dampness. She joined Nate on the other side of the vehicle, waiting as he gently lifted Lucy from the car seat and cradled her against his chest.

The sight of him holding Lucy as if she were something precious made her throat swell with emotion. Alex had once carried Lucy like that, until he allowed himself to get swept away with Debra's desire for a good time.

Nate would be a wonderful father someday.

They walked down the sidewalk toward her apartment building, Murphy on alert. Willow didn't relax until they were inside her unit with the door securely locked behind them.

"Put her on my bed," she whispered, leading Nate through to her room. Nate gently settled Lucy on the mattress, then stepped back. She drew the sheet up over her, then followed Nate back to the living room. Murphy was stretched out on the floor, resting his head between his paws. He looked content, as if he liked being there with her and Nate.

"Thank you." Tears pricked her eyes, the

events of the day abruptly overwhelming now that they were home.

"I shouldn't have suggested going to the park." Nate's blue eyes were dark with regret. "My carelessness exposed you and Lucy to danger."

"No, Nate. You saved us." She took a step closer, aching to reach out to him. "You put yourself at risk to shelter us."

"Willow." Her name was nothing more than a whisper, his blue gaze clinging to hers. They were both soaking wet from the storm, but that didn't matter.

She took another step forward and suddenly he pulled her into a crushing hug, burying his face against her damp hair.

His woodsy scent filled her with a mixture of peace and joy. Safety and excitement. From the moment they'd first met she'd longed for this. To feel his strong arms around her.

The cadence of his heartbeat matching hers.

Time hung suspended between them, enclosing them in a cocoon of warmth, until his phone rang. Nate sighed, then released her.

He glanced at the screen and grimaced. "My boss. I have to take this."

She nodded, unable to speak. Nate lifted the phone to his ear.

He ran a hand over his damp hair, his expression serious. She knew in that moment she was in trouble. Deep, deep trouble.

Because she cared about Nate Slater far more than she should. And knew, deep down, he'd only break her heart.

"A dead body?" Nate repeated, gathering his scattered thoughts. Making the leap from Willow's comforting embrace to yet another crime wasn't easy.

"Yeah, found in the alley behind the Burgerteria." Gavin's voice held a note of urgency. "There's a possibility this latest murder is related to whatever is going on with Willow Emery."

"Yeah." Nate glanced at Willow, still reeling from the near miss at the park. He found it incredible that she didn't blame him for what had happened. That she'd actually thanked him. "Was any evidence found at the scene?"

"Yep, a shell casing."

That pricked Nate's interest. He pulled the evidence bag from his pocket, looking at the one he'd picked up from the area where Murphy had alerted on Craggy Face's scent. "I have one from the park shooting, too."

"Good. We also have a witness." His boss had saved the best news for last. "I'd like you to get over there to interview him. Show him the guy in Willow's photo, see if he can ID him as the shooter."

Leave Willow and Lucy? Every cell in his body wanted to stay. But he couldn't ignore this potential link to finding Craggy Face. "Okay, but I need you to send someone here to watch over Willow and Lucy. It's clear they're still in grave danger. That gunshot was far too close."

"Yeah, okay. I'll send Vivienne and Hank. I have Ray and Abby on scene in the alley. They're waiting for you."

“Ray?” Nate was good friends with the narcotics officer and knew his springer spaniel was a great drug-sniffing dog. “Why send him to a homicide?”

“There’s a possible drug connection. You’ll find out more when you get there. Vivienne and Hank should be there in less than five minutes.”

“Got it.” He disconnected from the call and looked at Willow. Her apprehensive gaze made him feel bad. Was she upset about their embrace? Or because she knew he and Murphy had to leave for a while? He updated her on the situation.

“You really think this new murder is connected to me?”

He wasn’t sure how to respond. “I don’t know, but the location suggests a connection to the Burgerteria.”

“Craggy Face.” Her face went pale. “It all comes back to the stupid photo I took of Damon and Craggy Face.”

There had to be more behind this than a simple photograph, but he didn’t want to add to her concern. “Their involvement in something criminal isn't your fault, Willow. You just happened to be in the wrong place at the wrong time, with a camera."

"I don't understand. Is he coming after me because he thinks I have the camera on me?" Willow had given the camera to Nate as evidence in the case. "Or does he just want me out of the way because I can ID him?"

"I wish I knew." The escalating threats against her had to be related to something more than the photograph or camera. But what? "Listen, Vivienne and Hank will be here soon. I want you to think back to your time at the Burgerteria. The day you saw Craggy Face talking to your boss. Was there anything else going on that you can remember? Anything that may have seemed out of the ordinary?"

She shook her head, but then sighed. "I'll try, but nothing comes to mind."

"All I can ask is that you try." He smiled and moved toward the door. "I'll wait downstairs for Vivienne so the buzzer doesn't wake Lucy. Come, Murphy." The dog stretched, then joined him.

"Okay." Willow didn't move as he and Murphy crossed the apartment. There was no reason to feel as if he were abandoning her, yet it was difficult to keep walking, carrying her lilac scent.

He and Murphy took the elevator down to the lobby. They emerged just as Vivienne and her black-and-white border collie, Hank, arrived.

"Thanks for coming. I won't be long." He brushed past her, heading outside. The rain had stopped, but the air was thick with moisture, gray clouds hanging low.

He and Murphy walked the short distance, rather than risk losing his primo parking spot. As he approached the alley, he caught sight of a police SUV similar to his, parked so that the entryway to the back alley behind the building was blocked.

Edging past it, he and Murphy made their way to the crime scene. Murphy was on alert, his partner no doubt remembering they'd been this way before.

Ray Morrow and Abby were standing several feet from the dead body, next to a young kid wearing a bright yellow hoodie and carrying a skateboard. Probably their witness. As Nate approached, he could see the victim was lying facedown, his head turned to the side, a bullet hole in his back, in an eerie replica of how he'd found Willow's brother, Alex and his wife, Debra.

"Hey, Nate." Ray moved away from the guy in the yellow hoodie to meet him. He gestured to the dead man. "Vic's name is Paulie White."

Nate's gaze sharpened. "You know him?"

Ray nodded. "He's a low-level drug dealer. We've popped him a couple of times for intent to sell, but he never had more than a few grams of coke on him. He didn't play in the big leagues."

Nate crouched down to see the victim's face. The guy didn't look at all familiar to him. He glanced back up at Ray. "You don't think his murder is drug-related?"

"Maybe, but since we found the body here, Sarge wanted me to bring you in." Ray knelt beside him. "Interestingly enough, we found a brand-new top-of-the-line phone in his pocket. It's odd, because drug dealers lean toward using throwaway devices. Even better, we found a slip of paper in his pocket with a name and phone number."

A name and number! Nate felt a surge of adrenaline and rose to his feet. He and Ray took a few steps away from the victim. "I'd like to see it."

Ray handed him an evidence bag. The paper looked like it had been ripped from the bottom corner of a spiral notebook. The name *Carl Dower* was scribbled across the top, with a phone number written beneath.

"Did you run the name?" He looked at Ray.

"Not yet. I think that's why Sarge wanted you here. We also found this." Ray lifted an evidence bag holding a shell casing.

Nate pulled his shell casing out, too, comparing the two side by side. They looked identical, but he knew that alone didn't mean anything. They'd need the forensic team to prove they came from the same weapon. He handed the evidence bag to Ray. "Would you make sure the crime scene techs process both of these?"

"Absolutely." Ray took the bagged shell casing.

"What's the story with the witness?" He looked to where the kid was shifting his weight from side to side as if anxious to get out of there.

"Claims he was about to take a shortcut through here on his skateboard when he heard the shot." Ray gestured with his hand. "His name is Aaron Kramer and he just turned eighteen, so no need to wait for his parents to question him."

"Good. Come, Murphy." Nate strode to where Aaron waited.

"I already told the other cop everything I know. Can I go home now?"

"Just need a few more minutes of your time, and I appreciate your help." Nate smiled to put the kid at ease. "Would you mind starting again from the beginning?"

Aaron sighed heavily. "Like I told the other cop, I'd just turned the corner to cut through here on my skateboard when I saw this old geezer pull out a gun and shoot the skinny dude in the back."

"You saw the gunman's face?"

Aaron bobbed his head. "Yeah, man, it was freaky. Although I only saw him from the side, not directly."

A profile view was better than nothing. "Did he see you?"

"I don't think so. I immediately jumped off the board and ducked down behind that green dumpster back there." Aaron screwed up his face, then shook his head. "He didn't look in my direction, just took off that way," he added, pointing away from the dumpster. "I heard the sound of a car engine and assumed he had someone waiting for him. Man, he was in and out of here in less than a minute."

Less than a minute to kill a man in cold blood.

"Can you describe the guy?" Nate asked as he pulled out his phone.

"He was old and kind of heavyset."

Nate glanced at Aaron. "About how old?"

The kid shrugged. "I don't know. He had like wrinkles and stuff. Gray hair. You know, old."

The kid's description was far from helpful. He used his phone to call Eden, the unit's tech guru. "Hey, can you pull together a quick six-pack of mug shots for me to show our witness? Make sure they are all the same age and similar characteristics of Craggy Face and include his photo, too."

"Sure thing." Eden's fingers tapped on the keyboard of her computer. "Sending it now."

He heard the ping on his phone and pulled up the six-pack. Using a small phone screen wasn't ideal, but it would work in a pinch. He held the device toward Aaron. "There are six men here. Any of them look familiar to you?"

Aaron took the phone and used his fingers to enlarge each picture. To the kid's credit, he took his time. Then he nodded. "Yeah, man, this guy. He's the old geezer who killed the skinny dude."

Nate sucked in his breath. The witness had identified Craggy Face as the killer.

ELEVEN

Lucy awoke from her nap asking for her dolly. Willow gladly played with her niece, hoping the early-afternoon gunfire was long forgotten.

Vivienne and Hank helped keep Lucy occupied and for that Willow was grateful. When Vivienne's phone rang, Willow glanced over, wondering if the caller was Nate.

"Really?" Vivienne's eyes widened in surprise. "That's great news. Now we just need to find out the guy's name."

There was a brief pause as Vivienne listened, then the cop's knowing gaze met hers.

"Yes, I'll let her know. Thanks, Nate." Vivienne tucked the phone back in her pocket. "Nate stopped at his place to pick up a few things, but he and Murphy are on their way here now."

"What's the good news?" Willow unfurled herself from her seat on the floor.

Vivienne hesitated. "It's best if I let Nate fill you in."

Willow tamped down a flash of impatience. "I understand that there's only so much you can share about an ongoing investigation, but my life is in danger." She glanced down at Lucy, who was still seated on the floor with her doll. "Lucy's, too."

Vivienne nodded, her gaze solemn. "I know, but this is Nate's case. Sarge is letting him take the lead."

Her stomach clenched at the thought that Nate and Murphy would soon leave her in the care of other officers. Not that she could blame him. He'd been with her for well over twenty-four hours now. She was grateful for his protection and support, but sensed Nate wouldn't be happy unless he was in the center of an investigation, rather than watching from the sidelines.

"Sure." She forced a smile, then startled

when there was a knock on the door. She moved forward to answer, but Vivienne was faster.

"Let me." The K-9 officer peered through the peephole, then stepped aside, glancing at Willow with a frown. "Are you expecting a visitor?"

"No." Her stomach clenched with fear and she swiftly picked up Lucy from the floor. "Who is it?"

"I'll find out." Vivienne waited until she took Lucy into the bedroom.

Several tense seconds went by before Vivienne opened the door with a sheepish expression on her face. "It's Jayne Hendricks, Lucy's caseworker."

"Oh." Her shoulders slumped in relief, but then tensed again. This woman would be key in deciding whether or not she was an appropriate guardian for Lucy. She straightened her shoulders and followed Vivienne into the living area.

"Ms. Emery?" Jayne Hendricks looked to be in her late forties, with dark hair and glasses. Her deep brown eyes reflected a keen intelligence that made Willow believe she wouldn't be a pushover when it came to doing whatever was best for Lucy.

"Yes, I'm Willow, Lucy's aunt." She shifted the little girl in her arms so she could take Ms. Hendricks's outstretched hand. "It's nice to meet you."

"Likewise. And this must be Lucy." Ms. Hendricks's expression softened as she looked at her niece. "How are you, Lucy?"

Shy with strangers, Lucy hid her face against Willow's neck without answering.

"She's doing very well, considering." Willow forced a smile, wondering if she was required to tell the social worker about the recent gunfire at the park or the failed kidnapping attempt.

"I'm sure." Jayne Hendricks's gaze was compassionate. Then she glanced around the apartment. "You have a nice place here. Two bedrooms?"

Her stomach knotted again. "Just one. But I'm hoping to upgrade to a two-bedroom as soon as possible." She needed to get a decent price for her current apartment, but would that be enough to afford something larger? She tried not to panic.

"Hmm." The noncommittal response wasn't reassuring. Ms. Hendricks crossed the apartment, poking her head into the bedroom and then the bathroom.

Willow wondered if she'd get extra points for being a clean freak or if only having a one-bedroom apartment would be enough for this woman to decide to take Lucy away.

She tightened her grip on Lucy, who still hadn't said anything. No way was she letting this little girl go.

"How's Lucy coping?"

The question caught her off guard. "She had nightmares last night but calmed down when I held her in my arms."

"I'm sure it's a comfort to her to have you with her."

For the first time since the woman had entered her apartment, Willow felt herself relax. "Yes, I believe it's best for Lucy to be with someone she knows and loves. I promise I will do whatever it takes to care for my niece."

Ms. Hendricks opened her fridge, hopefully taking note of the chicken breasts and fresh broccoli she'd purchased the other day to make for dinner. Surely the healthy food had to be another point in her favor.

"I agree." Ms. Hendricks shut the fridge and turned to face her. "I think you're doing a wonderful job with Lucy and it's clear she trusts you."

"Thank you." Willow pressed a kiss against Lucy's temple, fighting tears of relief.

"Are you planning to adopt her?"

"Absolutely." She didn't hesitate. "I—just haven't had time to figure out how to go about doing that. I'm sure there's paperwork involved, right?"

"Yes. Our website contains all the information you'll need." Ms. Hendricks's gaze was warm now, and Willow felt certain that the paperwork would be little more than a formality. Her brother didn't have a will as far as she knew, but she was Lucy's only living relative. Ms. Hendricks held out a business card. "Call me if you have questions."

Willow took the card, tucking it in the front pocket of her jeans. “Thank you.”

Ms. Hendricks glanced at Vivienne and Hank, who were standing off in the corner. “I assume you’re here to protect them from the person responsible for murdering the Emerys?”

Willow froze. This was it. The moment of truth. Ms. Hendricks might decide to take Lucy away if she knew Willow was in danger from someone unrelated to her brother’s murder.

“Yes, ma’am.” Vivienne glanced at the doorway as Nate and Murphy entered the apartment. “There’s Detective Slater now. Members of our team are alternating the duty of watching over Ms. Emery and Lucy.”

Nate looked surprised to see the newcomer but quickly picked up on the fact that Lucy’s caseworker was doing a surprise home visit. He set a small duffel in the corner, then straightened. “Is there a problem?”

“No problem.” Willow’s voice was faint. She cleared her throat and injected confidence in her tone. “Detective Slater, this is Ms. Jayne Hendricks from Child Protective Services. She wanted to make sure Lucy was doing okay being here with me.”

“Understandable. The little girl has been through a lot.” He shook the caseworker’s hand. “Nice to meet you. I want you to know, we’re keeping a close eye on Willow and Lucy to keep them safe.”

“I can see that.” If Ms. Hendricks thought that having two sets of K-9 officers in her apartment was unusual, she didn’t let on. “Well, that’s all I need for now, but I’ll be in touch.”

Willow knew that meant she could expect another visit in the near future. Swallowing hard, she escorted Ms. Hendricks to the door. Even after the caseworker left, she couldn’t entirely relax.

“I feel guilty.” She looked at Nate. “I should have told her about the recent threats targeting me. Maybe Lucy is better off with a foster family.”

“Do you really believe that?” Nate’s tone was soft, gentle.

She instantly shook her head, resting her cheek against Lucy's wavy hair, breathing in the comforting scent of baby shampoo. "No. I'm afraid sending Lucy off with strangers would cause more harm than good."

"There's your answer." Nate turned toward Vivienne. "Thanks for your help. I'll take over from here."

"No problem. Come, Hank." Vivienne led Hank out of the apartment. Nate locked the door behind her.

"Doggy!" Lucy reached a hand toward Murphy. Now that the strangers were gone, she'd reverted back to her old self.

Willow set her on the floor, watching as her niece made a beeline for Murphy. Clearly, Lucy wasn't shy around Nate.

As Lucy gazed up at Nate in adoration, Willow realized her niece was growing emotionally attached to Nate.

And feared that his leaving once the danger was over would break the little girl's heart.

Nate quickly filled Willow in on the latest news on Craggy Face being identified as the shooter in the alleyway homicide case. "We're going to find him very soon." He opened his laptop and took a seat at the kitchen table. "I just need the guy's name."

"That is good news." Willow's smile was strained and he knew that being under the scrutiny of CPS had to be stressful. "I'm—uh, going to start dinner in about an hour or so. Are you planning to stay?"

He was surprised by her question. "Yes, unless this is your way of kicking me out?"

"No, of course not." She flushed and avoided his gaze. "I wasn't sure what your plans were."

His primary goal was to link Carl Dower—the name on the piece of paper found on the victim—to Craggy Face, so they could issue a BOLO for the guy. His secondary and no less important goal was to keep Willow and Lucy safe. He gestured toward his duffel bag. "I'm here until we find and arrest the man responsible for trying to hurt you."

"Thanks." Her smile was fleeting, and he frowned at the hint of sadness in her expression.

She put on some cartoons for Lucy, who enjoyed sitting beside Murphy while Nate searched for information on Carl Dower. He found a listing for the guy, and quickly dialed the number, only to discover there was no answer and no way to leave a message.

Drumming his fingers on the table, he tried to think of other ways to get a photograph of Carl Dower. He'd searched on social media to no avail. Was the eyewitness testimony against Craggy Face enough to get a search warrant for Damon Berk's records? He didn't think a simple photo of the two men together would be enough, especially since Berk claimed the guy had complained about a burger causing a cracked tooth.

In his gut he felt certain Carl Dower *was* Craggy Face. Too bad he couldn't find the evidence he needed to prove it.

Turning to the McGregor cold case helped distract him from failing to identify Craggy Face. He reviewed the notes, struck again at the similarities between the two cases.

His gaze lingered on photos of the brown

watch band that was found at the scene of the McGregor case. The DNA hadn't belonged to either of the victims. How good was the DNA testing twenty years ago? Certainly not as meticulous and thorough as it was now. Surely it had been tested again more recently.

Or had it?

Reaching for his phone, he called Gavin. "Sarge, when was the last time we had the watch band retested for DNA?"

He could hear the shuffling of papers on the other end of the line. "Five years ago, but you raise a good point. Could be someone has been arrested in the years since. I'll get the forensic team on it."

"Sounds good. Let me know if you get a hit."

"You and the entire team will know the minute I do," Gavin promised.

"Still nothing from the Emery crime scene?"

"Nothing outside the parents. Their DNA is all over the place."

"Yeah." He sighed. "Okay, thanks." Setting his phone aside, Nate thought about how impossible it seemed that the McGregor killer hadn't struck again in the five years since they'd had the DNA tested, or if he had, had been smart enough not to leave one iota of DNA behind.

As the evening wore on, Willow busied herself in the kitchen cooking dinner. He tried to ignore her, but the simple fact was that no woman had ever cooked for him.

Not him, he swiftly corrected himself. Willow was cooking for Lucy. He and Murphy didn't belong here.

Yet somehow, he felt more comfortable sleeping on Willow's sofa than he did in his own place. Shaking his head at his foolishness, he startled when his phone rang.

"Slater."

"Nate? It's Darcy from the forensic team. I have good news."

"I'll take it." At this point any evidence would be welcome. "What did you find?"

"The two bullet casings Ray dropped off from the attempt at Owl's Head Park and Paulie White's murder in the alley at Burgerteria are a match. They're the same make and caliber and have the same markings indicating they are from one gun, a thirty-eight to be exact."

One gun. He turned the information over in his mind. He had to believe that Craggy Face had shot and killed Paulie White after the attempt on Willow at the park. Or was it possible he'd used the weapon at the park, then handed the gun to an associate who'd gone after Paulie? The timing seemed almost too close.

"Do we have a time of death on Paulie White?"

"Not yet. ME's not doing the autopsy until the morning, but the tox screen will take several days. At least we know the same gun was used on both crimes."

"Yeah, but within a narrow time frame." He tried to estimate how much time he and Vivienne had spent at the crime scene at the park. Ninety minutes? Was that enough time for Craggy Face to hightail it back to the Burgerteria to nail Paulie? And if so, why had he killed a low-level drug dealer?

That piece of the puzzle really didn't make any sense.

"Hey, are you still there?"

He pulled his thoughts together. "Yeah, thanks, Darcy. Appreciate the heads-up."

"I'll let you know if I come up with anything else."

"Thanks. Oh, do you know when Willow can have access to her brother's place? She still needs to pick up Lucy's things."

"Maybe tomorrow. I'll check with my boss and let you know when we're ready to release the scene."

"Thanks." He set his phone aside, still grappling with the timeline between the shootings.

"Dinner's ready."

He hastily put his computer away to make room at the small table for the meal. The scent of Italian seasoning made his mouth water. Willow put Lucy in her booster seat, then set the baked chicken, marinara sauce, noodles and cheesy broccoli on the table.

"What's that?" Lucy pointed at the cheesy broccoli.

"Little trees and cheese. They're yummy." Willow's tone was encouraging.

"Little trees are my favorite," he declared, helping himself to the broccoli. Lucy had tried the scrambled eggs when he'd said that, so he was hoping she'd do that again.

"Just a small bite," Willow cajoled.

Lucy obliged, then smiled. "Little trees are my favorite, too."

"The cheese helps," he whispered as Willow cut the chicken into bite-size pieces.

"Exactly." Willow smiled wryly. "Not sure she's had much exposure to veggies. I appreciate your help encouraging her to try the broccoli."

"Hey, it is my favorite." He tried to keep his tone light, even though this sharing a meal together felt too cozy for his peace of mind.

This—being together—couldn't amount to anything. He wasn't father material and refused to be tempted by something he couldn't have. In fact, he wanted to spend more time on the Emery murders. The minute they had Craggy Face in custody, he'd have to move on. The McGregors had waited twenty years without answers; this new murder with the same MO had to be investigated for a potential link. Besides, Willow and Lucy deserved justice for the loss of Alex and Debra.

His life revolved around putting bad guys in jail. Not playing happy homemaker with Willow and Lucy.

As soon as they'd finished eating, he went back to work on his laptop. Willow cleaned up the kitchen, gave Lucy a bath, then tucked her into bed. He found himself listening as they said their nightly prayers.

"God bless Aunt Willow, Detective Nate and Murphy," Lucy said. "Amen."

"Amen," Willow echoed. "Good night, Lucy. I love you."

"I love you, too."

His throat closed with pent-up emotion. Listening to them only reinforced his role of being on the outside, looking in. He shut his laptop with a sigh. Carl Dower was nowhere to be found, and the phone number remained a dead end, too. He stood, stretched, intending to lie down on the sofa, when Willow emerged from the bedroom.

"Hey." She offered a wan smile. "I'm too keyed up to sleep. Thought I'd make some chamomile tea."

"I'm not much of a tea person. Does it help?"

She lifted a shoulder. "Sometimes." After filling the teakettle, she placed it on the stove. "It can't hurt."

Silence engulfed them as she waited for the water to boil. When she'd filled a mug with steaming water, she came into the living room to sit beside him on the sofa.

"What made you choose to become a K-9 cop?" She cradled the mug in her hands as if absorbing the warmth. She'd asked that question the first night he'd stayed over, and he'd found himself talking more about his colleagues' reasons—only the ones who were open about it—than his own.

"Oh, well, that's kind of a long story." One he normally didn't talk about.

Willow looked embarrassed. "Sorry, I

didn't mean to pry into your personal life. I get it's none of my business."

"No, really, it's okay." He felt bad for making her feel guilty. If anyone deserved to know about his past, Willow did. They'd grown close over the past thirty-six hours, and he thought telling her about his past might help her understand him better. "There was a cop, a guy named Geoff Cally, who came to our rescue the night my mom and I managed to escape my dad."

"Escape?" Her brow furrowed, her cinnamon gaze searching his. "He hurt you?"

"Yeah." He instinctively reached up to massage the collarbone his dad had cracked that night. The bone had healed, but the pain lingered in his mind. The shock of being hit hard enough to slam into the wall, to break a bone. "My father drank a lot and took his anger out on my mom. I was a skinny kid, ten years old, when I decided to fight back."

"Ten." Her voice was a horrified whisper. "Oh, Nate."

He shrugged off her sympathy. "That's all in the past now, but that night Officer Geoff

Cally came to our aid, arrested my dad and had us taken to the hospital, then a shelter." He thought back to the horror of that night, going to the hospital, then being moved to a shelter. "He didn't just drop us off and forget about us. He returned to check up on us, to make sure we were okay. He eventually helped us find an apartment of our own." The place had been a dump, but he'd felt safer there than he ever had in the house they'd lived in with his dad. "He was truly an amazing guy."

"A role model that made you want to become a cop, just like him."

He couldn't deny it. "I went to the academy and placed in the top of my class. I worked the beat for a couple of years, then heard about an opening in the K-9 unit." He reached down to stroke Murphy's soft coat. "I'd always wanted a dog, but, well..." He shrugged. "The competition is stiff. I wasn't sure I'd be chosen, but thankfully I was accepted into the program. I worked in another unit for a few years, and was recruited for the new Brooklyn team. I like working for Gavin Sutherland, and with the rest of the crew." He hesitated, then added, "They're the only family I'll ever have now that my mother is gone."

"What do you mean?" Willow frowned.

He shook his head. "I haven't lost my temper yet, and I don't drink, but there are times I feel the anger simmering deep inside." He forced himself to meet her gaze. "I can't risk having a family of my own, Willow."

"Oh, Nate." Her compassion was nearly his undoing. "You're nothing like your father. You've been nothing but sweet and kind to Lucy, and I think you'd be a wonderful dad. And don't forget, God is watching out for you."

She didn't know what she was talking about, but he couldn't find the words to correct her.

Willow scooted over to him, placed her hand on his arm, heat radiating from her fingertips. Then she bent over to kiss him. He was sure she'd meant it to be a chaste, healing kiss, but that wasn't the case. Their lips clung, then meshed. He drew her into his arms, deepening their kiss.

"Aunt Willow!" Lucy's plaintive cry had them springing apart. "The mean clown is back."

"Excuse me." Willow hurried into the bedroom to comfort Lucy from her nightmare, leaving him gasping for breath, wrestling with the realization that his feelings for Willow were not that of a cop whose duty was to protect her, or even that of a friend.

No, he cared about Willow on a personal level, far more than he had a right to.

TWELVE

The impact of Nate's kiss made it difficult to sleep. Willow had stared blindly up at the ceiling for an hour, emotions spinning in turmoil. Her heart ached for the young boy who'd been beaten by his father, who'd escaped with his mother to live in shelters. She thanked God for watching over them, and for bringing a man like Geoff Cally into Nate's life. The cop had not only helped keep Nate and his mother safe but had been a wonderful role model for Nate.

Yet Nate didn't think he deserved a family of his own. And hadn't mentioned God or faith. Because he didn't believe? The thought made her sad. And avoiding a family wasn't the right path; he would make a wonderful husband and father.

But not for her and Lucy. That much had been made clear.

After a restless night, she slid from the bed early, doing her best not to wake Lucy. But by the time she'd finished in the bathroom, Lucy was sitting in the middle of the bed, sleepily rubbing her eyes.

"Good morning, Lucy." Willow crossed over to give her niece a hug.

Lucy hugged her back, more clingy than usual. "I hav'ta go to the bathroom."

"This way, remember?" Willow took her into the bathroom, grabbing a new outfit for her to wear so she could change out of her jammies. When Lucy was set, they returned to the kitchen.

"Are you hungry? I'm making French toast for breakfast."

Lucy frowned. "I like regular toast."

"Do you like maple syrup?" When Lucy nodded, she smiled. "Then trust me, you'll like French toast, too. Come on, you can help."

"Is Murphy here?" Lucy looked up at her with wide, hopeful eyes.

Hearing his name, Murphy got up from his position on the floor next to the sofa where Nate was stretched out and came over to greet Lucy, tail wagging, licking her face. She giggled and threw her arms around his neck.

"I love Murphy."

"I know, baby." She glanced over at Nate, who was wearing sweatpants and a T-shirt, his blond hair mussed from sleep. Gold whiskers dusted his cheeks, making him look rugged and somehow even more attractive.

Do. Not. Remember. His. Kiss.

"French toast for breakfast." She cleared her throat and headed into the kitchen. When she lived alone she'd never cooked this much, especially since she spent her days making gourmet burgers in her job. But now she knew Lucy needed structure, to know when her next meal would be.

No more living with uncertainty. Bad enough that her niece was haunted by nightmares. As she whipped up the egg mixture for French toast, it occurred to her she should have asked Ms. Hendricks to recommend a child psychologist. She made a mental note to call her later.

Nate took Murphy outside, returning after a few minutes. “Lucy, will you play with Murphy while I take a shower?”

“Yes.” Lucy looked thrilled with the idea.

By the time Nate returned, the French toast was finished. She put out a plate for Lucy, cutting the toast in bite-size pieces.

“Thanks, Willow, this is great.” Nate’s praise made her cheeks go pink.

“You’re welcome, but it’s truly not a big deal.” She took a sip of her coffee. “Have you learned anything new about Craggy Face?”

“Not yet.” Nate glanced at her. “But I do need to head out for a while. I’d like you and Lucy to stay inside with the door locked.”

She paled at the thought of being here without Nate and Murphy watching over them. “Alone?”

“I’ve arranged for someone to hang out here for a bit.” He avoided her gaze and she wondered if he'd made these so-called arrangements after their kiss.

The one she was not going to remember.

"Vivienne?" She didn't mind having female company but wondered how the officer felt about being assigned to babysitting duty.

"No, another colleague of mine, Noelle Orton." He glanced at his watch. "She's a rookie, but a very good one, and our boss is keeping her off the streets for a while since her K-9 partner has a bounty on her head for being too good at her job. Noelle should be here within the hour."

"Okay." She told herself to get over it. So what if they would be stuck inside for a few hours? Keeping Lucy safe was all that mattered. She forced a smile. "We'll find something fun to do."

"Listen, Willow. Darcy, the forensic tech assigned to your case, is checking with her boss to see if they'll release your brother's place sometime later today." His gaze was full of compassion. "I know you're anxious to get more of Lucy's things. When I get the okay, I'll take you over there to pick out what you'd like."

"I would love that and I'm sure Lucy will be glad to have more toys to play with, too." She was touched he'd thought of it. "Thanks, Nate."

He nodded and quickly finished his breakfast. She wanted to ask what he was planning to do, but doubted he'd be able to tell her.

All she could do was pray that he and Murphy would be safe.

"I'm full," Lucy announced. "Can I watch cartoons?"

"Yes, but only until I'm finished with the dishes." She wiped the sticky syrup off Lucy's hands and face, then took her into the living room to turn on the promised cartoons.

"I like this one." Lucy plopped in front of the television.

"That's fine." At least the show would keep her niece mesmerized for a while.

She returned to the kitchen to find Nate

had already cleared the table. "I'll help with the dishes."

"There's no need. I can handle it."

"I don't mind." He filled the sink with sudsy water. "You keep feeding me, so it's the least I can do."

She decided there was no sense in arguing. They worked side by side in silence for several minutes, listening to the cartoons in the background. Murphy stretched out on the floor in front of Lucy.

"Lucy is going to miss Murphy when you're gone." She glanced at him as she dried a plate. "I'm going to miss both of you."

Nate's hands went still in the water for the space of a heartbeat. "Willow, I feel like I need to apologize for kissing you last night."

She lifted a brow. "I'm fairly certain I was the one who kissed you."

The tips of his ears turned red. "Regardless, I should have stopped you. I told you about my father, Willow. As much as I care about your safety, there can't be anything more between us."

In other words, no more kissing. It wasn't anything she hadn't already told herself but hearing him say the words caused a pang in the region of her heart. "I understand, but I believe God is watching over you, Nate. He'll always be there for you, no matter what."

"I'm not sure I believe that." His words sounded guttural, almost harsh. "God wasn't there when my father slammed me into the wall or punched my mother in the face."

She sucked in a harsh breath. "Oh, Nate. I know how horrifying that must have been for you, but don't you think that God had a hand in sending Geoff Cally to save you and your mom that night? That God asked Geoff to look out for you, to keep you both safe?"

He shook his head, but she saw a flash of uncertainty in his eyes. "Maybe."

She wanted to say more but decided to let it go for now. When Nate finished washing the dishes, he turned to her. "You could be right."

Her heart soared with hope. "You're always welcome to attend church services with us next weekend."

She expected an instant refusal, but he slowly nodded. "Maybe. Depends on what's happening with the case."

No point in pushing, because she knew that for cops, firefighters, nurses and doctors, sometimes church services had to be skipped while on duty.

But as Nate went over to put Murphy on his leash, she hoped and prayed that he'd find a way to attend church with her.

If there couldn't be anything personal between them, she'd find a way to live with that. But she refused to accept the idea of Nate living his life without God's strength and support.

Where in the world was Noelle? Nate desperately needed to get out of the apartment, to get some distance from Willow and Lucy.

The moment he'd woken up to see Willow standing there, he'd wanted to pull her into his arms and kiss her again. To breathe in her calming lilac scent.

Now she was talking about God and asking him to go to church with her and Lucy. And he'd practically agreed.

What was wrong with him?

He headed for the door. "I'll be right outside. I'm sure Noelle will be here soon."

She nodded and he quickly stepped into the hall before he could do something he'd regret.

Like kiss her goodbye.

His phone rang and he pounced as if it were a lifeline. But the caller wasn't Noelle, it was fellow K-9 officer Lani Jameson. Lani was married to Noah Jameson, the current chief over the NYC K-9 Command Unit in Queens. With a protective brother on the team and her husband running it, Lani had transferred to the Brooklyn K-9 Unit the moment she heard about recruitment efforts. Nate had met Lani a few times on the job and had always considered her to be a good cop.

"What's up, Lani?"

"I need your help. I just saw a skinny stray dog that looks a little like Snapper—she definitely has some shepherd in her—and I think she's recently given birth. I'm worried about her puppies and where they might be. Can you spare some time right now?"

The entire NYPD knew about Snapper's history. The beautiful German shepherd had once been partner to Jordan Jameson, Noah's older brother and the former chief of the NYC K-9 Command Unit. The dog had gone missing after the chief was murdered, and when they'd finally found the K-9, he was partnered with Lani, particularly to keep Snapper in the Jameson family. In Nate's humble opinion, the two of them made a great team.

"Sure, I'll help," Nate said. "But I need to stop at the Burgerteria after. I have more questions for the manager. Where are you now?"

"I'm in Sunset Park." She gave her exact location. "Where are you?"

"Bay Ridge. I'll meet you in twenty minutes." A beep indicated he had a second call. "See you soon." He switched over to the new call. "Noelle?"

"I'm here in the lobby." The rookie officer sounded cheerful.

"Thanks, Noelle. I really appreciate this. Come on up to apartment 706."

"Got it." The call ended.

When Noelle arrived, he introduced the petite, dark-haired officer to Willow and Lucy, trying not to squirm beneath Willow's all-too-knowing gaze. She seemed well aware that Nate really needed some space.

After leaving Willow in Noelle's care, it didn't take long for him to meet up with Lani in Sunset Park, a neighborhood that offered a nice view of the Statue of Liberty.

"This is where I saw the stray last," Lani explained, gesturing to a wooded area of the park. "I think she's hiding her pups somewhere close by. I'm worried she'll be picked up by the humane society or that the puppies will die."

He had to admit, he didn't like the sound of that, either. "Okay, let's spread out a bit, see if one of our K-9s can flush her out."

Only a few minutes went by when he heard Lani's urgent call. "Nate! Over here!"

He broke into a run, catching a quick glimpse of the skinny shepherd trotting past about twenty yards away. Lani had her phone out to snap a picture before she headed toward the stay. "Here, girl."

The skinny shepherd glanced at them, then began to run.

"Hurry, we're going to lose her! I need to find those puppies!" Lani and Snapper ran faster.

He and Murphy tried to close the gap, but as they came out from beneath a large tree, he abruptly stopped. "Where did she go?"

Lani stopped, too, breathing hard as she scanned the area. "I don't know. She was right there!"

He turned in a circle, noting they were in the corner of the park where it butted up against two other neighborhoods: Borough Park and Windsor Terrace. "Do you think she crossed the street? There's nothing but residential housing on the other side."

"I hope not. What if she gets hit by a car?" Lani sounded worried.

"Maybe she's just hiding."

"I shouldn't have stopped for a picture, but I was hoping to share this with the rest of the team, so we could all be on the lookout for her." She sighed. "Poor dog. I just hope her puppies are okay."

"I'm sure they will be. Listen, we can try looking for her again later, but I have to go. There's some legwork yet I need to do on my case."

"I get it." Lani sounded dejected. "Next time, I'm coming out here with a small steak."

That made him smile. "Should do the trick."

Lani shared the dog's photo with Nate and sent one to Eden Chang as well to be dispatched to the rest of the team. She also texted the Brooklyn Animal Care Center to be alerted to check for puppies in the park if the stray was brought in. "I'm calling her Brooke, short for Brooklyn."

"I like it."

They made their way back to where they'd left their respective vehicles. Nate fought stop-and-go traffic heading back to Bay Ridge. He wanted to push Damon Berk a bit more about Craggy Face. Maybe once Berk knew the guy was wanted for murder, he'd change his tune about the guy complaining about a cracked tooth.

Nate wanted to know the true nature of their conversation.

When he finally reached Bay Ridge, he circled around several blocks before he found a parking spot. He let Murphy out of the back and clipped his leash before walking down toward the Burgerteria.

The restaurant had just opened for business and the early lunch crowd was seated on the various tables inside. Several of the patrons eyed Murphy curiously as he scanned the interior searching for Damon Berk.

One of the servers, wearing a name tag that identified her as Salina Alden, finally approached. "I'm sorry, but we don't allow dogs in here. It's a health hazard."

"I need to speak to Damon Berk."

"He's not here. He left me in charge." Salina frowned. "Why do you want to talk to Damon? Is this about the guy who was found dead in the alley behind the restaurant yesterday? Everyone has been talking about it all day."

Good guess. He wasn't surprised the news had spread like wildfire. "You're positive he's not here? Maybe you could check his office to make sure."

Salina rolled her eyes. "I'm telling you, he's not here and hasn't been all morning."

Nate wondered if Berk was avoiding the place because of the recent murder. Without a search warrant, he couldn't poke around, looking for something, anything, that may explain why Willow had become a target and Paulie White had been murdered. He pulled out a business card. "Will you call me when Damon returns?"

Salina reluctantly took the card. "I guess so. But Damon doesn't know anything about that murder. None of us do."

"Paulie White didn't work here?"

"No!" Her eyes widened in horror. "Of course not."

"You didn't notice anything out of the ordinary yesterday?" He figured the uniforms had already canvassed the area, but was stalling for time, hoping Damon might show.

"Nothing. We were super busy, running around like chickens when we heard the shot. Even then, we thought maybe it was a car muffler or something."

Brooklyn was noisy, but he felt certain the shot would have sounded loud even in here. "I'd like to talk to the staff working in the kitchen. They may have noticed something prior to the shooting."

Salina didn't look happy but did as he requested, bringing the kitchen workers out to talk to him. He performed quick interviews of the dishwasher and the cook who'd replaced Willow, but they both claimed they didn't see or hear anything.

By the time he was finished, Damon still hadn't shown. And for all he knew, Damon had taken off somewhere with Craggy Face. Or maybe he was hiding from the guy. Nate decided to pick up something for lunch on his way back to Willow and Lucy when his phone rang.

"Hey, Sarge," he greeted his boss. "Tell me you have good news."

"We finally located the O'Malleys."

It took a moment for Nate to place the name. "The landlords who own the home Alex and Debra Emery rented, correct?"

"Yeah. Apparently, Belle tracked them on vacation in Florida. They acknowledged that the Emerys were five months overdue in their rent, and claim they were going to put them on eviction notice when they returned but deny having anything to do with the murder." There was a pause before he added, "Their alibi is rock solid, Nate. They're in the clear."

He'd run out of leads to follow in both of his cases, leaving him cranky and frustrated.

How much longer before Craggy Face struck again?

THIRTEEN

Willow enjoyed playing with Lucy, but she couldn't deny feeling on edge, even with the female officer there, as she waited for Nate and Murphy to return. When her phone rang, she eagerly grabbed the device, her heart thudding when she saw Nate's name on the screen.

"Hi, Nate."

"Hey, Willow. I'm on my way back with a basket of chicken for lunch. Hope that's okay."

She was pleased he'd thought of the little girl. "Thanks."

"My boss also confirmed he released the scene at your brother's house. He gave us the okay to head out to pick up what you need for Lucy."

"That's wonderful news." Lucy was already getting bored with her doll, and she would be glad to have more of Lucy's things to help the little girl feel at home.

"See you soon."

"Okay." She disconnected from the call and set her phone on the table, glancing over to where Noelle Orton was seated on the far end of the sofa. "Nate's on his way back. I'm sure you're getting sick of sitting around doing nothing."

The petite rookie officer looked surprised. "Protection detail is part of my job and I'm happy to be here."

For the first time, she realized how seriously Nate's team was taking the threat against her. She suppressed a shiver and strove for a light tone. "Well, thanks for spending your morning with us." She glanced at Lucy, who was playing with some blocks on the rug. "Time to wash our hands, Lucy. Detective Nate will be here soon."

"Yay! I miss Murphy," Lucy said, and followed her aunt to the bathroom.

Just as Lucy was drying her hands, Willow heard footsteps outside the apartment door and then Noelle opening the door for Nate. The little girl rushed out to say hi.

"Hi, Pipsqueak." Nate's welcoming smile and cute nickname warmed her heart. "I brought chicken for lunch." He glanced at Noelle. "For you, too."

"Thanks." Noelle joined them at the table. Willow put Lucy in her booster seat while Nate unpacked the chicken.

"What did Damon have to say about Craggy Face?" Willow asked as they all began eating.

"Damon didn't go in to the restaurant today, so I didn't get a chance to talk to him." He glanced at his watch. "I've located his home address. I'm planning to head over there later. But first, we can take a trip to East Flatbush to pick up Lucy's things."

Willow wanted to protest. The idea of Nate going to confront Damon at his home worried her. Sure, he was a trained cop and had a great partner in Murphy. But still, she didn't like it.

"Maybe Noelle should go with you." The

words popped out of her mouth before she could think about them.

The two cops exchanged a look. "I'll be fine," Nate said. "Noelle has other duties, I'm sure."

Noelle finished her chicken, balled up the wrapper and stashed it in the bag. "I need to get back to Liberty, but if you need me, let me know."

Nate scowled. "I won't."

Willow grimaced. She shouldn't have overstepped. "Thanks again for coming over to sit with me, Noelle."

"Not a problem." Noelle waved her gratitude. "Thanks for lunch, Nate, but I gotta run." The officer said goodbye to Lucy and then left the apartment.

"You don't have faith in my ability to manage Berk?" Nate asked with a frown.

"I do. I just..." She hesitated, unwilling to say too much. "I don't want you to get hurt." *Or killed.* The image of her brother and his wife lying dead on the living room floor flashed in her mind.

"I'm done!" Lucy's voice was a welcome intrusion. "I wanna get down."

Willow dabbed the girl's face with a napkin before lifting Lucy out of the booster seat.

"Ready to head out?" Nate asked as he helped her clean up the table.

"Sure." She glanced down at Lucy, wondering how her niece would take this. Maybe she could ask Nate to stay with Lucy in the car while she went in to get what she needed.

She helped Lucy wiggle into a light jacket, then the little girl got into the stroller.

Outside, the air was cool after the rainstorm the day before. She kept a tight grip on Lucy's stroller.

"My SUV is this way." Nate walked beside her, his body placed in a way that protected her from anyone driving past on the street. Murphy kept pace beside him, his nose sniffing the air.

When they reached Nate's police vehicle, she was secretly glad when he stood protectively behind her as she placed Lucy in the car seat. Only after they were both settled safely inside did he put Murphy in the back and slide in behind the wheel.

"Do you really think Damon will talk to you?" She couldn't help ruminating on his plan to confront her former boss.

Nate shrugged, his gaze focused on the traffic. "It can't hurt to try. For all we know, he's hiding from Craggy Face."

"Maybe." She thought back to the day she'd taken photos of her gourmet burgers. It seemed like eons ago instead of mere weeks. Had the conversation between Damon and Craggy Face held a note of animosity? She didn't think so. But then again, she hadn't paid close attention to the conversation, her eyes on the lens.

As they drove, she fell silent, dread forming in her gut as Nate brought them closer to her brother's home. Like scenes from a movie, she remembered hearing the squeaky black iron gate swing open, seeing the front door hanging ajar, hearing the sounds of Lucy's sobs.

Finding her brother and his wife, dead.

Nate pulled up to the curb and she forced herself back to the present. The house looked just as forlorn and unkempt as before—worse now, maybe, because of what had transpired within the four walls.

Before Nate could speak, she looked at him. “I think you should stay in the car with Lucy while I go inside to get Lucy’s things.”

He frowned. “No way. You stay here while I go.”

“But I know where everything is.” She didn’t really want to go inside, but felt as if it was her duty to pick out the things Lucy needed.

“Is her room on the second floor?” She nodded. “I’m sure I can find Lucy’s clothes and toys. Stay here, please.” His blue eyes were mesmerizing as they pleaded with her. “Maybe you can play a game to keep Lucy occupied.”

She twisted in her seat, looking at Lucy, who was putting her fingers up to the crate and giggling as Murphy licked them. She nodded, deciding it was best for the little girl. “Okay.”

Nate reached over to gently squeeze her hand before he got out of the car. He let Murphy out of the back and approached the house.

Her hand tingled from where he'd touched it. She told herself to stop being foolish. Nate had made his stance perfectly clear. There couldn't be anything between them.

Other than friendship.

Nate carefully moved through the crime scene, heading up the stairs to the second floor with Murphy at his side.

His partner sniffed around the room, no doubt recognizing Lucy's scent. Nate tried to think like Willow, choosing outfits that matched, then poking through her toys. He found another doll and some large pink, orange and white Legos. He stuffed as many items as he could fit inside a large plastic bag before making his way back down to the main level.

The crime scene was still marked with dried blood, but the rest of the house remained the same. He thought again about the mess, wondering if the killer had been searching for something. If Darcy or anyone on the team had found anything suspicious, like drugs or money hidden someplace inside, they'd have let him know. Either the killer had found it, or the items had been hidden somewhere else.

He knew the crime scene techs had taken dozens of samples to test, a task that would likely take weeks to complete. And what they had tested so far had come up with a big fat nothing.

Tamping down a stab of frustration, he reminded himself that the forensic team members were excellent at their job and would eventually find something that would help them solve the case.

He hauled the bag outside, glancing up and down the street as he made his way toward the SUV. A black sedan, looking much like the one that had been stolen and used in Willow's kidnapping attempt by Craggy Face, was coming toward them, driving much slower than the rest of the traffic.

His pulse spiked and he quickened his

pace, closing the gap between him and the car. “Willow, get down!”

Willow’s pale face stared blankly at him for a moment, then she unlatched her seat belt and climbed over the console into the back seat. She curled her body protectively around Lucy in her car seat.

He understood her need to protect the little girl, but he hated knowing they were both in danger yet again.

Nate pulled his weapon, pointing it at the black sedan, tracking it as it crawled forward. He caught a glimpse of a deeply lined face behind the wheel, but then the driver pulled a cap down low and abruptly stomped on the gas.

The black sedan lurched forward.

“Stop! Police!” Nate’s shout caused several other drivers to look around as if trying to figure out who he was talking to.

The black sedan rolled past. He wanted to shoot at the tires, but there were people crossing and so he held back for their safety.

He stared at the license plate, which was

covered in mud. Despite the dark smears, he could just make out the last two letters, *EM*.

He opened the back hatch. "Jump, Murphy."

His partner leaped inside the crated area. He slammed the back shut, then rounded the vehicle to get into the driver's seat, taking a moment to toss the plastic bag of Lucy's things in the passenger seat. He gunned the engine, flipped on the red-and-blue lights, and pulled into traffic.

It was illegal to have your license plate obscured, unable to be clearly seen, an offense he could use to pull the driver over and issue a citation. If it was Craggy Face, all the better. He didn't like following the guy with Lucy and Willow in the back seat, so he quickly keyed his radio.

"This is Unit Ten requesting backup. I'm heading southwest on Linden Boulevard following a black Lincoln sedan, license plate mostly covered with mud, the last two letters Edward Mary."

"Ten-four," the dispatcher responded.

"There's a patrol located about a mile east. I've directed them to your location."

"Copy." Nate kept his gaze on the sedan. The driver ignored his lights, darting the Lincoln among cars to put more distance between them. Nate did his best to keep up, not wanting to lose him, yet unwilling to engage in a full-out chase with Willow and Lucy riding in the back seat.

"Hurry. He's getting away." Willow's voice was low and intense.

He briefly met her gaze in the rearview mirror. "I can still see him. Backup will be here shortly."

"But I think it's Craggy Face! And he's getting away." Willow looked distraught over the possibility.

The black sedan made another cut over to the left lane, the driver he'd cut off punching the horn in a display of irritation. Nate did his best to keep pace without putting them in danger, desperate not to lose him.

"He's turned!" Willow's voice rose in panic.

Nate pushed his foot harder on the accelerator, cars moving out of his way as they realized he wasn't interested in pulling them over, but in following someone else.

Seconds later, he reached the same intersection, turning left. But when he looked up ahead, he didn't see the black sedan.

No! He couldn't have lost him!

"Look right, tell me if you see him." Nate kept his gaze on the streets off to the left. There were several black cars, but no Lincoln sedan.

"He's not this way from what I can tell." Willow's voice was low and hoarse, as if she were fighting tears. "But there are lots of places to hide."

He couldn't disagree. Still, he kept going straight, hoping he'd find the sedan. He reached for his radio. "Subject turned off the boulevard, and I haven't been able to pick him up. Any hits on a black Lincoln with a license plate ending in Edward Mary?"

"Let me send you to Eden, she's searching for a possible match."

"Thanks." He ground his teeth together, vying for patience.

"Nate? I have a report of another stolen vehicle, a 2013 black Lincoln sedan." She read him the license plate, ending with *EM.*

"Stolen?" He couldn't believe it. "When?"

"Earlier this morning, same MO as the previous theft. Owner is Joe Keene. He works for Keene, Carmel and Banks, a law firm. He claims he came home just after midnight and didn't realize his car was gone until late the following morning." Eden's voice held remorse.

"Get a BOLO out for the vehicle. I want every cop in the entire borough looking for it."

"Understood." He heard Eden's fingers tapping on her computer keyboard. "I'm bringing up all cameras in the Linden Boulevard area. Maybe we'll find him."

"Yeah. Call me if you do." Nate dropped his hand from the radio, resisting the urge to slam his fist against the steering wheel.

He couldn't believe he lost him. That his backup hadn't arrived in time. Sure, Eden might be able to pick him up, but he knew it was likely that the driver, if it was Craggy

Face, would ditch the stolen vehicle as soon as possible.

"We lost him." Willow's voice was little more than a pained whisper.

Her disappointment stabbed deep. Remorse burned hot, churning in his belly. This was the second time he'd failed her. First when he'd been lured away by a fake crime, barely returning in time to prevent Craggy Face from kidnapping her, and now this.

He couldn't allow a mistake like this to happen again.

FOURTEEN

Lucy's sobbing had eventually eased, but knowing her niece was calm didn't make her feel any better. Willow knew that the black sedan with the muddy license plate had been there because of them. A close call that could have ended much worse if Nate hadn't shown up when he did. Despite how much she'd wanted clothes and toys for Lucy, it wasn't worth the risk.

She wished she understood why Craggy Face was after her. None of it made any sense and she was growing weary of constantly being under surveillance and protection.

The sooner Nate and his team found and arrested Craggy Face, the better.

Nate's grim expression held a note of self-recrimination. As if this was his fault, when she'd been the one to ask to come back for Lucy's things.

From now on, she knew she needed to stay inside the apartment with Lucy. No more outings, no matter how stir-crazy they became from being cooped up inside.

"I'm taking you and Lucy home," Nate said, interrupting her thoughts. "I never should have allowed you to come along."

"None of this is your fault, Nate. God was watching over all of us, and thanks to you and Murphy, you scared him off."

Nate gave a sharp shake of his head in a frustrated gesture but didn't argue. They rode in silence back to her apartment building in Bay Ridge. Ironically, the black sedan had taken them in the direction of her home.

And the Burgerteria.

It seemed all roads led back to the restaurant where she'd worked for three years. Three years! And never a hint of anything illegal going on related to Damon Berk, or anyone else for that matter.

She rested her head against Lucy's car seat, battling a wave of exhaustion. Logically she knew her fatigue was just the aftermath of the adrenaline rush, but she also hadn't been sleeping well.

Mostly because Lucy had been plagued by nightmares of her parents' murders. The little girl often moaned about the mean clown and repeated over and over again she didn't want the monkey.

Willow wasn't sure how to reassure Lucy that taking the stuffed monkey from the bad clown didn't mean she was responsible for the death of her parents. She thought again about Penny McGregor and the rapport she'd established with her niece. Maybe she could get Penny to come back to talk to the little girl again.

Nate pulled into a parking spot and shut down the engine. He turned in his seat to look at her. "Murphy and I are going to escort you and Lucy inside first. I'll bring up your things later."

"Okay." She took Lucy out of the car seat, holding her close as she slid out of the vehicle. Nate's strong arms surrounded her and his woodsy scent helped calm her nerves.

The trip to her apartment was uneventful. Nate left Murphy on guard as he retrieved the plastic bag, along with his computer.

As she unpacked, putting Lucy's things into dresser drawers, Nate remained hunched over his computer. When she'd finished creating a toy corner for Lucy, she crossed over to see what he was doing.

"That's a nice building," she said, looking at the elegant apartment building on the screen. The building looked new.

"Yeah, the real question is how does Damon Berk afford to live there?"

Good point, although her building was nice. Not new and fancy, but decent. "Maybe, like me, he had money from an inheritance."

"Maybe." Nate didn't sound convinced. He continued various searches. "Check this out. The owner of the new apartment building Damon lives in is a guy by the name of Oscar Banjo. Banjo also owns the building that houses the Burgerteria and that new place you were talking about the other day, the Basement Bargains store."

A shiver snaked down her spine.

Nate's gaze was fixated on the screen as he continued to search. "Banjo isn't our Craggy Face, though. Here's a photo of him at the ribbon-cutting ceremony. That's him, standing beside Theresa Gray, deputy mayor of housing and economic development."

She bent over his shoulder to see the screen more clearly. Oscar Banjo was young, in his thirties. Younger than she'd thought to have amassed such a fortune. "Definitely not our Craggy Face."

Nate pulled a chair over and gestured toward it. "No, but it is interesting that he owns the building the restaurant is in. Sit down, Willow. I need you to think hard about whether or not you remember seeing this man in the restaurant, maybe before you took those photos."

She dropped into the chair, her gaze fixated on the screen. There was something familiar about his features, but she couldn't place where she'd seen him. "I can't say for sure, but he may have been in the restaurant."

"Take your time," Nate urged. "You have a photographer's eye. Think back to those weeks leading up to the day you took the photos of your gourmet burgers."

She didn't want to disappoint him, and she really, really wanted to help put Craggy Face behind bars. But as she stared at Oscar Banjo's face, she simply couldn't say for certain when he'd been in the restaurant. His features were ordinary, nothing that would have captured her artist eye.

"I'm sorry, but I can't say for sure." Her shoulders slumped. "I wish I could, but I can't. There's nothing about this guy that would have captured my attention. He could be one of hundreds of customers that came in and out of the restaurant each day."

"That's okay. Thanks for trying." If Nate was frustrated, he didn't show it. "Interesting that he's so young. This guy is being touted as one of New York's up-and-coming real estate moguls. He just turned thirty-six last month."

"Yeah, but again, that doesn't prove anything." She wasn't sure where Nate was going with his comments. "I'm sure he made a couple of investments that happened to pay off."

"Or he has someone backing him up," Nate countered.

She swiveled in her seat to stare at him. "Are you insinuating he's part of the mob?"

He lifted his hands in a gesture of surrender. "I'm not insinuating anything. It's just a theory." His gaze returned to the screen. "I'm going to keep digging for a while, see if I can find anything that links Banjo to Craggy Face, aka Carl Dower—or at least I'm pretty sure that's his name. It was written on a slip of paper found on the drug dealer Craggy Face killed."

She nodded and rose to her feet. She trusted Nate to find Craggy Face. More, she trusted Nate with her life and Lucy's.

When Nate's phone rang, she jumped, looking over at him expectantly. His expression was serious as he listened. "Okay, thanks, Eden."

"What?"

"They found the stolen Lincoln, abandoned not far from Prospect Park. They're checking for prints, but..." He shrugged.

Disappointed, she sighed. Craggy Face was too smart to leave fingerprints behind.

Although she wished she knew why he was so intent on causing her harm.

The rest of the evening passed by uneventfully. Lucy was happy to have her princess pajamas that Nate had brought from her brother's house.

Willow lay beside Lucy to tell her a story but felt herself dozing off, her niece snuggled against her.

"I'll kill you and the brat, too!"

"No! Please, Lord, save us!" Willow ran and ran, through the alley, dodging around dumpsters, her breath heaving from her lungs, her pulse thundering in her ears.

Nooo.

She awoke with a jolt, her face wet with tears, hardly able to breathe from the tightness of her lungs. She swiped at her face, reminding herself it was only a dream.

A terrible, horrible dream.

Taking care not to wake Lucy, she slipped

from the bed and made her way to the bathroom. She splashed cold water on her face, trying to erase the images in her mind.

"Willow? Are you all right?"

She dried her hands and face and opened the bathroom door. Nate stood there, looking rumpled from sleep, yet still far too attractive for her peace of mind. Murphy stood beside him, looking up at her as if he were worried about her, too. "Yes. I'm sorry I woke you."

"I heard muffled crying, thought it was Lucy." His gaze was dark with concern.

"It was me. I—had a nightmare." She shivered. "But I'm fine. Thankfully I didn't wake Lucy."

"Come here, sit down for a minute." Nate took her hand and led her to the sofa. Murphy flopped on the floor at their feet. "Do you want something? Water? Tea?"

His offer was sweet, but she shook her head. "No, thanks. I'm fine."

He sank down beside her. "You want to talk about it?"

She blew out a breath. "It was just Craggy

Face chasing me, telling me he was going to kill me and Lucy." The images her mind had conjured up had been all too real.

Nate put his arm around her shoulders and drew her close. She reveled in his warmth. "I won't let anything happen to you, Willow. You and Lucy are safe with me and Murphy."

"I know. God is watching over all of us." She leaned against him, burying her face against his T-shirt. He was a rock in an otherwise stormy sea. "I just want this to be over. For Lucy to be safe."

"I know." He brushed a kiss to her temple.

Nestled against him, she didn't want to move. Somehow, in the short time she'd known him, Nate had become important to her. More than a friend, despite her best efforts to hold him at arm's length. He was so wonderful to her and to Lucy, she just knew he'd make a wonderful husband and father.

After several long moments she lifted her head, searching his gaze in the dim light from the city flowing through the living room window. "You're a good man, Nate Slater," she whispered.

He shook his head, but his gaze clung to hers. "You don't know how often I wrestle with my anger."

She tipped her head to the side. "Don't we all wrestle with our flaws? Mine happens to be impatience, in case you haven't noticed. None of us is perfect, Nate, but God loves us anyway."

He didn't say anything, his gaze thoughtful. She leaned up to kiss him on the cheek, even though she'd rather have a real kiss from him.

He flashed a wry smile and hugged her. For a moment she clung to him, wishing for something more. As she pulled away, his mouth captured hers and she couldn't stop from kissing him the way she'd wanted to.

But then she forced herself to pull away, knowing that this was the path to heartbreak. Her breathing was ragged, but she managed to pull herself together. "Good night, Nate."

He released her and she thought she could

feel his gaze boring into her back as she moved toward the bedroom.

As she slipped back inside the bedroom she shared with Lucy, she heard his whisper.

"Good night, Willow."

No surprise that Nate didn't sleep well after Willow's mind-blowing kiss. The words she'd told him had echoed over and over in his head.

He'd found himself wondering if God had been looking out for him and his mother, bringing Geoff Cally into their lives to help save them.

That God was actually helping him to keep a tight rein on his temper. To be fair, he'd never lost it, but he'd always assumed it was a matter of time.

He'd caught a few hours of rest until Willow and Lucy had gotten up. He took care of Murphy first, then when they were finished in the bathroom, he took his turn.

Willow was making scrambled eggs when he emerged. Lucy had her doll sitting on the chair beside her and was trying to convince her aunt to give her dolly some breakfast, too.

"She can share some of yours, Lucy." Willow glanced at him with a smile. "Good morning, Nate."

"Morning." He cleared his throat and took the seat across from Lucy. "I'm going to head out for a while today, but I'll arrange someone to come and stay with you."

The light in Willow's cinnamon eyes dimmed but she nodded. "Okay. Breakfast will be ready in a jiffy."

"Thanks." He was humbled by how easily she included him in meals, so he made an effort to keep Lucy entertained as she cooked.

"Who's coming to babysit this time?" She placed a plate with eggs and toast in front of Lucy, then brought him a larger serving.

"I'm waiting to hear back." He'd made the call while outside with Murphy. He didn't want to leave her alone, but knew his preoccupation with Willow and Lucy had to stop. "The team is busy this morning, and if one of them can't come, then I'll get someone from the closest precinct to come over."

"Okay." Willow joined them at the table.

When they'd finished eating, Nate helped clean up the dishes, then made another call to his unit. There was still no one available for protection duty, so he made the call to the nearest precinct. Their boss had to talk to Gavin before they agreed to send a female cop, Kathleen Kuhn, over.

She arrived almost thirty minutes later. She didn't look happy about the assignment, but he didn't care. Finding Damon Berk and/or Craggy Face was his top priority.

And he couldn't do that while sitting here in Willow's apartment. As it was, he was getting a later start than he would have liked. Still, he forced a smile. "Thanks for coming, I really appreciate it."

"Yeah, sure." He didn't let her lack of enthusiasm get to him. "What's your phone number, in case I need to reach you?"

He rattled it off, then entered her cell number into his phone, too. He put Murphy's vest on, then straightened. "I'll be on the radio, too." He turned and headed to the door. "Come, Murphy."

Murphy was on alert as they left Willow and Lucy with Kathleen. Despite her attitude, he felt certain the cop would take protecting Willow and Lucy seriously.

Willow's apartment wasn't far from the Burgerteria, so he headed there first. He wasn't leaving until he'd confronted Damon Berk about Craggy Face and the murder of Paulie White.

The restaurant was supposed to be open by ten thirty in the morning, according to the hours posted on the door, but as he and Murphy approached, the interior was dark, no sign of customers seated inside. He tried the door, but it was locked.

He frowned, a sliver of apprehension snaking down his spine. Were the employees running late? Or was something deeper amiss?

He leaned in close, cupping his hands around his face so he could see better. At first there was nothing, then a dark shadow of movement. The figure turned and he instantly recognized Damon Berk.

"Hey! Berk! Open up! Police!" He rapped sharply on the door, holding his badge up so that Damon could see it. The manager looked indecisive for a moment, as if he wanted to run, then reluctantly approached.

He opened the door just enough to talk. "Now what do you want?"

"Why are you closed?"

Damon scowled, sending a furtive glance over his shoulder as if seeking reinforcement. "My delivery truck is late. Can't make burgers without ground beef. I'll be opening soon. Why does it matter to you?"

It didn't but he'd wanted to get the guy talking. "Listen, your buddy Carl Dower is wanted for murder." His blunt statement seemed to catch Berk off guard.

"What? Wait a minute, he's not my buddy." Panic flared in Damon's eyes.

"How did you know who I was talking about, then?" Nate challenged. "The guy who you were talking to in the photograph Willow took was Carl Dower, right?"

"No, I—uh, well, I may have remembered his name from when he complained about his food, but that doesn't make him a friend." Sweat beaded along Berk's hairline again. Nate couldn't contain a surge of satisfaction that he had Berk right where he wanted him.

"If you don't want to be arrested for aiding and abetting a known felon, you'll tell me where to find him."

"I don't know." Berk's denial sounded weak.

A flash of movement from behind Berk caught his eye. "Who's back there? Is that him? Dower?"

"No!" Berk blocked the doorway with his body, closing the door even further. "It's the cook. I told you my food shipment is late."

Nate didn't believe him. Murphy growled low in his throat, his nose working as he sniffed the air, and that was enough to convince him. He whirled away from the restaurant door, instinctively knowing Dower had headed out the back. "Come!"

He raced down the road, around the corner leading to the back alley running the length of the building. Murphy kept pace, although he knew his partner could easily outrun him.

As he headed down the alley, he could make out a figure dressed in black up ahead. It wasn't easy to tell from the back, but Nate felt certain it was Carl Dower. "Get him, Murphy!"

Murphy put on a burst of speed, easily closing in on the guy.

The perp suddenly stopped and turned. A gun! No! Dower was pointing the weapon at Murphy!

"Heel, Murphy! *Heel!*" Nate reached for his weapon, hoping, praying that he could stop Dower from shooting his partner.

The command caused Murphy to stop on a dime. His partner turned and came back toward him. The sound of a gunshot echoed sharply, ricocheting off the buildings surrounding them.

"No!" His voice was hoarse as he returned fire. "Murphy!"

He was so focused on his partner that he

didn't realize that Dower had fled the scene. He dropped to his knees, gathering Murphy close, feeling for any sign of an injury.

No blood, thankfully. Nate sent up a quick prayer of thanks to God for watching over his partner.

He rose to his feet and ran to the end of the alley. But it was too late.

Dower was gone.

FIFTEEN

Nate called for backup, frustrated with himself for letting Carl Dower escape. While he waited for someone from his team to arrive, he ran around to the front of the restaurant and pounded on the glass door. "Berk! Open up!"

The manager didn't answer. Nate wondered if the manager had taken off once he and Murphy had gone around back, or if he was hiding inside. His gut leaned toward hiding. He yanked on the door, but it was still locked.

"Berk!" He shouted and pounded again, but there was still no response. Reeling in his temper, he spun away from the door and reached for his phone.

"Roarke? It's Slater. I need your help." Henry Roarke was a K-9 detective who was stuck on modified desk duty while IAB investigated an excessive use of force allegation, a claim no one believed for one minute. Roarke wasn't happy about the situation, annoyed with how long it was taking the IAB to clear his name, but being on desk duty meant Henry was in a good position to do the paperwork he desperately needed in order to get a search warrant for the Burgerteria.

After explaining to Henry what he needed, the K-9 detective sounded hesitant. "I don't know, Nate. Dower isn't in the restaurant now. He took off. I'm not convinced a judge will approve this. After all, you don't know for sure that Dower was inside the restaurant, right? You didn't see his face until he was in the alley. All we can say is that Dower may have been in the restaurant but was for sure in the alley."

"I know it was him." He scowled and rubbed his jaw, replaying those tense minutes when he'd caught the flash of movement. He let out a heavy breath, knowing he couldn't lie. "But you're right, I didn't get a good look at him inside the restaurant."

"Listen, I'll do my best," Henry promised. "I'll call you back as soon as I hear something, okay?"

"Yeah, thanks." He disconnected from the call and returned to the alley just as Vivienne and her K-9 partner, Hank, approached.

Nate jogged over to meet them. "Carl Dower was here—around back. He fired a gun at Murphy and took off on foot. We need to find him!"

"Did you call Eden to look for camera footage? He may have gotten on the subway or at least close enough to be picked up on the subway cameras."

Good point. He reached for his radio. "Dispatch, I need to talk to Eden." He waited for the dispatcher to transfer the call, scanning the alley. "Vivienne, call the crime scene techs. If possible, I'd like Darcy to come look for the brass left behind from Dower's weapon."

"Will do." Vivienne reached for her phone.

"Chang," Eden answered through the radio.

"It's Nate. I need you to look at the cameras near the Burgerteria restaurant, see if you can pick up Carl Dower, aka Craggy Face, you know, the guy you found on video before. He took a shot at Murphy."

"Oh no! Is Murphy okay?"

Nate glanced down at his partner. "Yeah, he's not hurt. Thankfully Dower missed."

"Okay, let's see. I have five cameras up around the area you've mentioned. Here!" Her voice lifted in excitement. "I found him! He's still on foot, about seven blocks from you, heading east. You better hurry, the camera on the next block is broken. He's heading into a video dead zone."

"I'm going. Come, Murphy!" Nate broke into a run, envisioning the streets in his head so he could find the shortest route. His police SUV was located in the opposite direction, so he didn't bother to go back for it.

"I'll try to head him off at the pass in my vehicle." Vivienne shouted from the driver's seat. "Stay on your radio!"

He barely spared her a glance as he ran for all he was worth. He knew Dower was armed but couldn't tolerate the idea he might actually get away.

Nate wanted, needed to find him. To toss him behind bars where he belonged.

He made good time, but as he reached the intersection, there was no sign of Dower. He called Eden, breathing hard. "Do you have him on video?"

"No. I'm sorry, but he's gone." Eden's voice echoed with regret. "He never showed up on any of the other cameras after heading into the radius of the broken one. I have to assume he once again was picked up in a vehicle."

"How is that possible?" Nate bent over to brace his hands on his knees. Murphy nudged him with his nose, then licked his face. He slowly straightened, raking his gaze over the area. "Do you think he knew this particular camera was broken?"

"Maybe, but I'm not sure how. It's not general knowledge available to the public, but who knows if he has friends in high places? I'm sorry, Nate. I feel terrible that I lost him."

"It's okay." He sighed. The broken camera was hardly her fault; in a city the size of New York, there was no way to avoid the occasional broken camera. Still, it nagged at him that Dower had managed to disappear in the black void.

"I'll keep scanning for him. Maybe I'll be able to pick him up again."

"I hope so." Nate disconnected, then turned to retrace his steps to go back to the Burgerteria, Murphy keeping pace beside him.

His phone rang and he quickly picked it up. "Slater."

"It's Vivienne. I'm stuck in traffic. Have you found him?"

"No. Eden lost him, too. Broken camera." He tried not to sound as disappointed and upset as he felt. "I'm heading back to the Burgerteria. Hopefully Henry can get the search warrant I requested."

"Nate, Sarge wants us to report to headquarters. He wants an update on this case

ASAP. He didn't like hearing Murphy was almost hit by a bullet."

The last thing he wanted to do was to leave the scene of the crime. But if their boss wanted an update, he didn't have any choice but to comply. "Okay, fine. I'll be there soon."

"Later." Vivienne ended the call.

Nate broke into a light jog. Instead of going to the restaurant, he went to where he'd left his SUV. Murphy needed water, and the backs of all their K-9 vehicles were equipped with a fresh water system, a key component in taking good care of their four-legged partners.

He had to trust that Darcy would find the brass left behind by Dower's gun.

Once they found the guy, he planned to charge him with attempted murder of a police officer, adding to the long list of crimes the guy was guilty of perpetrating.

Additional crimes they no doubt had yet to uncover.

What had Dower been doing with Damon Berk in the back of the restaurant? Was it possible he'd threatened Berk? If so, with what? Did Dower have something to hold over Berk's head? Was the sweat beading on Berk's face more of an indication of fear, rather than nervousness at getting caught doing something illegal?

He didn't know and that bothered him. The only clue they had to why Willow and Lucy were in danger was related to the stupid photograph. Unless…he straightened in his seat. Unless Dower and Berk thought she knew more than just what she'd captured on film.

Like what? He had no clue.

But the possibility wouldn't leave him alone.

Willow tried to ignore Officer Kuhn as she played with Lucy. The female officer was nice enough, but not nearly as friendly as Vivienne, Noelle and the other members of the K-9 unit.

The ones she knew were more like family to Nate and Murphy.

Not that being nice and friendly really mattered as long as she and Lucy were safe.

As the hour approached noon, Willow pushed herself to her feet. "I'm making grilled ham and cheese sandwiches for Lucy's lunch. Would you like one?"

"No, thank you." Officer Kuhn's tone was polite, yet distant. "I'm vegan, so I ordered online from a local vegan restaurant that delivers."

"Okay."

"Aunt Willow, I hav'ta go to the bathroom!" Lucy suddenly jumped up from the floor, so Willow led her into the bathroom.

She heard a thudding noise from the apartment and thought it was likely that Officer Kuhn's vegan lunch had arrived.

"I'm hungry," Lucy said as Willow helped her wash her hands.

"Lunch will be ready soon, honey." Willow used the towel to dry Lucy's hands. "You need to clean up your toys while I grill our sandwiches."

The door to the bathroom abruptly opened, hitting her sharply in the elbow. "Hey!" She turned toward the doorway, annoyed that Officer Kuhn had barged in. But it wasn't the female officer at all.

Craggy Face stood in the doorway, his expression grim with a mixture of anger and satisfaction. She noticed his face was flushed and sweaty, his overall appearance disheveled. Had the man run here from somewhere? He held a gun in his hand, the muzzle pointed at her chest. "Don't move or I'll shoot."

Her pulse spiked, her mouth desert dry with fear and loathing. How had he gotten in her apartment? Where was Officer Kuhn? She felt trapped in the tiny bathroom yet managed to find her voice. "What do you want?"

Lucy began to wail. "Bad man with a gun!"

"Shh, it's okay." Willow didn't take her gaze off Craggy Face but reached down to pull Lucy up and into her arms, cuddling the little girl close and smoothing a shaky hand over her hair. "Stop it! You're scaring her."

"You should be scared. Move it." Craggy Face stepped back, waving his gun in a way that indicated she needed to come out of the bathroom. Dressed in black from head to toe, baseball cap on his head, he looked menacing and all too capable of carrying out his threat. Willow didn't want to leave the sanctuary of her apartment, but what could she do? There was no way to outrun a bullet.

If it were only her being held captive, she might have taken the risk. But she couldn't put Lucy in danger.

It was her duty to keep the little girl safe.

Dear Lord, help us! Please, keep us safe in Your care!

The prayer helped calm her nerves. Nate and Murphy were out there. They'd figure out that she and Lucy were missing and would do everything in their power to find her.

Craggy Face locked a hand on her arm, squeezing so tight she winced. The cold barrel of the gun pressed into her side. "We're walking out of here nice and easy, understand? If you say or do anything to get someone's attention, I'll shoot you and deal with the consequences."

"Wh-why?" She forced the words past the tightness of her throat. "Y-you have the photographs. What more do you want?"

"It's not what *I* want." His breath was hot against the side of her face and reeked of onion. She tried not to gag. "It's what the boss wants. Let's go."

He shoved her hard and she stumbled, nearly losing her grip on Lucy. As much as she didn't want to leave the child alone, she couldn't bear bringing her into the center of danger. "Hold on, Lucy will slow us down. Let me leave her here."

Craggy Face sneered then shrugged. "Hurry!"

"Stay here, Lucy, okay? You'll be safe." She put Lucy down. It wrenched her heart to listen to Lucy's sobs as she closed the bathroom door to keep the little girl inside, but knew it was for the best.

She gasped when her desperate gaze landed on the prone figure of Officer Kuhn, lying in an unconscious heap on the floor, blood seeping from a wound on her temple.

"Wait! She needs medical attention!" Willow dug in her heels, trying to stall for time. Maybe Nate would contact Officer Kuhn, and then rush over here when she didn't answer her phone. "We need an ambulance."

"No." Craggy Face dug the gun barrel into her side, making her suck in a breath as pain shot through her midsection. She tried to shrink away from the gun barrel but couldn't. "Move it! Or you'll be sorry."

She moved as instructed. Craggy Face pushed her into the hallway and closed the door behind them. He didn't take her onto the elevator, though, shoving her instead toward the stairwell.

"Not a word," he warned.

She swallowed hard and nodded. She continued repeating her silent prayer, hoping someone else would come upon them in the stairwell. That someone would notice there was something wrong and call the police.

But as they went down one set of stairs

after another, taking all seven floors down, they didn't see anyone. And when they reached the lobby, Craggy Face wrapped his arm around her shoulders, as if he were comforting her, while the barrel of the gun pressed painfully in the soft tissue beneath her rib cage.

Remembering the cameras in the lobby, she glanced upward, attempting to telegraph her fear with her eyes without raising Craggy Face's suspicions. Yet even as she did her best, she knew it may be hours until anyone watched the video footage.

At which point it may very well be too late.

When they stepped outside, her hope of being discovered evaporated into a fine mist. Pedestrian traffic was brisk; summer tourists crowded the streets. Everyone was in a hurry, no one paying attention to the woman being ushered down the street by a man old enough to be her father.

Maybe they assumed Craggy Face *was* her father.

She glanced from person to person, trying to make eye contact in an effort to let someone know there was something wrong.

But no one appeared to notice.

"Wh-where are we going?" Her voice was hoarse with fear.

"I told you." The onion breath was strong, and she couldn't help wrinkling her nose beneath the assault to her senses. "To meet the boss."

The boss? She frowned. "Damon?"

Craggy Face let out a harsh laugh. "Not hardly. This is all his fault in the first place. If that idiot doesn't watch out, he'll be dead meat, too. This is his last chance to make things right."

Dead meat, too. The boss. Not Damon Berk. Willow managed to put one foot in front of the other, following Craggy Face's orders with a sick sense of dread. She felt as if she were walking toward her execution and didn't know how to stop it.

She truly didn't understand what was going on. Something criminal, clearly, but what? The photograph had been of Craggy Face. What about that had gotten her to this point? To the assault on a police officer? To being dragged out of her apartment at gunpoint?

To this man being so willing to shoot her in cold blood?

SIXTEEN

"I really want to get inside that restaurant." Nate looked at his boss, Sergeant Gavin Sutherland, seated across the table. "All roads lead to the Burgerteria."

Gavin nodded. "Henry's working on the search warrant…but I haven't heard back yet."

They'd gathered in the large conference room located on the second floor of their precinct. He'd only been there for thirty minutes and was itching to get back out to the alley. Darcy hadn't found the bullet casing yet, but he knew it had to be there somewhere.

Although getting the casing and matching it to the others they'd found wouldn't necessarily convince a judge to sign off on the search warrant. They needed more.

He put his hand down to stroke Murphy's soft fur, forgetting they'd all kenneled their partners for the meeting. Gavin had requested a rundown, which he'd given as succinctly as possible.

"Anything else?" Gavin asked.

"No. That's it." Nate hesitated for a moment, then added, "Listen, I need to go." He couldn't ignore the itchy feeling crawling up his spine. "I want to get back to the Burgerteria in case the search warrant comes through. And if it doesn't, I still might be able to convince Damon Berk to cooperate."

Gavin leveled a steady glare at him, as if silently warning him not to go off the rails. "Fine. But keep me updated on what you're working on. I don't want to hear about an officer nearly being shot from the dispatcher."

He couldn't stop in the middle of a pursuit to contact his boss, but he understood Gavin was more upset about Murphy's close call than angry with him.

"I will." He surged to his feet and left the conference room. Down on the main level, he freed Murphy from his crate and headed back outside. He drove straight to the Burgerteria, intent on getting through to Damon Berk.

He knew, deep down, that somehow the restaurant was the key to cracking the case.

His phone rang. Officer Kuhn.

He pulled over to the curb, double-parking in a spot near the entrance to the alley. His heart thudded painfully in his chest as Kathleen said in a groggy voice, "Willow is gone. I— He hit me. I lost consciousness but when I came to, she was gone and the kid was closed up in the bathroom. I'm sorry."

Who had grabbed Willow? Even as the question formed in his mind, he knew it was Craggy Face. Carl Dower. "Stay with Lucy, will you? I'll call for an ambulance and backup." He disconnected from the call, quickly called dispatch and jumped out of the SUV. After taking Murphy out of the back, he ran to the back side of the restaurant.

Rounding the corner, he caught a glimpse of Willow being pushed in the rear door of the restaurant by Dower.

No! His chest was so tight it hurt to breathe. He reached for his radio. "I need backup in the alley behind the Burgerteria! My prime suspect, who I believe is Carl Dower, has kidnapped Willow."

"Ten-four. Backup on the way."

He and Murphy ran down the length of the alley, his mind grappling with the fact that Willow was inside with Dower. He couldn't wait; he needed to go after her right now. There was no need for a search warrant; these were exigent circumstances. A crime in progress.

Weapon in hand, he paused at the door, taking a deep breath to steady his nerves before easing it open.

Please, Lord, keep Willow safe!

The prayer rose from his heart, reaching for the sky as he entered the building with Murphy at his side. The idea of Willow being harmed made it difficult to concentrate. He kept his partner off leash, knowing that they would need every advantage in order to get Willow out of there, alive and unharmed.

Inside the building, he noted a steep staircase leading down into a basement storage area. Terse voices echoed off the concrete, but the words weren't easy to understand.

Holding his breath, he eased down on the first step, expecting a loud creak or groan of the wood to give him away. Hearing nothing but the staccato beat of his heart, he eased down a second step. Then a third, hugging the wall and holding his weapon ready.

Using hand signals, he instructed Murphy to stay at his side. As he drew closer to the bottom of the stairs, the words from the men below became clear.

"Why is this my fault?" Damon Berk's nasal voice was distinctly familiar. "You're the stupid idiot who shot Paulie right behind the restaurant over a stupid phone. What did you think would happen? Of course the cops came here looking for you."

"Paulie was threatening to talk! And it's your fault because of her!" The lower, husky voice had to be that of Carl Dower. "You encouraged her to take those pictures! Now the boss wants our heads on a platter!"

"She was supposed to take pictures of burgers, not people!" Damon's nasal voice turned whiny. "How was I to know she was some sort of amateur photographer? And would find your ugly mug interesting!"

"That photo is on the wall of the community college for everyone to see!" Dower's low voice rose with anger. "I grabbed it, but not until it had been posted for days. All because of you!"

"You need to convince the boss it was her fault, not mine," Damon whined.

Nate wondered if Damon and Carl were the only two men down there, or if there were others, possibly someone standing guard over Willow. He took another step. The wood beneath his boot creaked and he froze, his heart lodged in his throat. He signaled for Murphy to stay and leveled his weapon, prepared for the worst.

The seconds ticked by slowly. Eventually, he let out his breath in a soundless sigh. The two men were arguing loud enough that they must not have heard him.

Every cell in his body wanted to rush to

Willow. But he forced himself to remain calm. Nate took another step and noticed there were several large boxes piled along the wall in front of him. He thought they must contain food or other restaurant supplies, but then he caught a glimpse of a popular phone logo along the side.

What in the world? He frowned, trying to understand why the basement of the Burgerteria would contain boxes of expensive phones, when it clicked. The expensive new phone that Paulie White had.

This wasn't about drugs, as he'd originally suspected, but about stolen goods.

Involving enough money to kill for.

Willow huddled as far from Craggy Face and Damon Berk as she could get within the confines of the small space. The entire basement was filled with boxes of various sizes and shapes, containing items like high-end televisions, laptop computers and phones.

There was even a box of cameras just like hers.

She tried not to worry about Lucy, hoping

the little girl was safe in the apartment. She backed up to a stack of boxes and leaned against them for a few moments. She knew Craggy Face had brought her here to face their boss, but he hadn't let a name slip.

While the men had argued, she tried to reach for her phone again. She pushed the buttons on the screen without looking, estimating the numbers 911, but without success. The call didn't connect. She tried again, and when that didn't work, she edged the phone out further and glanced down at the screen.

No service.

Swallowing hard against a shaft of disappointment, she slipped the phone back in her pocket. Being surrounded by concrete must have made it impossible to get a cell signal.

The stairs were to her left and a little behind her. Maybe if she could get to the staircase leading up to the main level, she could make a run for it.

Maybe.

The image of being shot in the back caused a shudder to ripple through her. But what option did she have? She couldn't just stand here waiting for the boss to arrive.

For all she knew, the boss planned on killing her anyway. Might as well try to escape before that happened. Especially since the two guys were intent on their argument.

Willow sent up a silent prayer, asking for God to give her the strength she needed to get out. Feeling calmer, Willow eased away from the boxes and took a tiny and silent step to the side, toward the stairs.

She thought about what Nate had said about his childhood. She understood his perspective a little better now. Being in danger like this, knowing Craggy Face was armed with a gun, made it difficult to believe. But she refused to give up hope. Deep down, she knew God was watching over her, and that He would send Nate, or another cop, to save her, too.

"I'm going upstairs to wait." Damon's statement caused her heart to sink in her chest. She didn't want to be left alone down here with Craggy Face.

In her heart she didn't believe Damon was

a killer, but there wasn't a single doubt in her mind that Craggy Face could pull the trigger, shooting her in the blink of an eye.

"You're not going anywhere." Craggy Face took a menacing step toward Damon. "We're waiting right here, understand?"

Damon shrank from the older man. "Yeah, uh, sure, Carl."

Willow took another step, her gaze glued to Craggy Face. Had he noticed her movement? He continued threatening Damon Berk until the man was practically cowering in the corner, his face buried in his hands.

Now! She turned and ran toward the stairs.

"Hey! Stop or I'll shoot!" Craggy Face's voice held a note of panic.

She didn't stop. She hunched her shoulders, expecting to feel the sharp impact of a bullet at any moment.

A dark shadow moved from the landing of the stairway, and she feared she was too late. That their boss, whoever he was, had come down without her hearing him.

But then she recognized Nate and Murphy. She knew it! Her heart soared in her chest. She knew he'd come!

"Get behind me." Nate grabbed her arm and quickly shoved her behind him. She heard a sharp retort ring out, followed by a second gunshot.

No! She stumbled, almost going down to the concrete floor at the thought of Nate being hit. She tried to turn back, to see what had happened.

Nate lowered his weapon, his expression grim. Damon was on the floor, curled in a ball, his arms covering his head. "Don't shoot, I'm not armed, don't shoot!" The sobs came from deep within, and she almost felt sorry for her old boss, even though she knew he was complicit in the crimes Craggy Face had committed.

Craggy Face swayed, his hand pressed to his bleeding chest, a look of surprise on his face. As if in slow motion, the gun in his hand fell from his grip, clattering loudly against the cement floor. "You shot me." The words came out in a surprised tone as he slowly sank to the floor.

"Stop! Police!" The shout came from up above and suddenly there were several cops thundering down the stairs to the basement. She had to move out of the way to give them room to get by.

"Nate? Are you hurt?" She raked her gaze over him, searching for injuries.

"I'm fine, but the box of phones isn't." He gestured toward the bullet hole that had gone into a box mere inches from where he stood. She understood he'd had no choice but to shoot Craggy Face in self-defense. Nate abruptly stepped forward, pulling her into his arms. "Are you all right?"

Her knees went weak as the initial rush of adrenaline began to fade. "I—think so. Scared, but not hurt. But I had to leave Lucy in the bathroom…" She swallowed a sob.

"Lucy's okay. Officer Kuhn has her."

She closed her eyes on a wave of relief. "Leaving her behind was the hardest thing I've ever done. I need to call Officer Kuhn."

"Of course."

She reached for her phone but once again,

there was no service. She'd need to wait until they were up in the alley.

One of the cops pressed a towel to the bleeding wound in Craggy Face's chest while another cuffed him just in case. The officer then handcuffed Damon Berk, as well. Damon didn't protest; in fact, he almost seemed grateful to be with the police, his eyes red and puffy from crying.

It was over.

"Let's get out of here." Nate's voice was low and husky in her ear.

She nodded, forcing herself to step away from the warmth of his arms. Without hesitation, she headed up the stairs.

In the alley, she was about to pull out her phone, but then saw Office Kuhn and Lucy standing near several police officers.

"Lucy!" She rushed forward to take her niece into her arms. "I'm so happy you're okay." She lifted her gaze to the injured officer. "Thank you so much."

"I'm the one who owes you an apology." Kuhn's expression was contrite. "She kept crying and the ambulance crew felt we were both fine, so I thought it best to bring her to you."

"Thank you." Tears pricked Willow's eyes.

Nate came over to join them, his expression mirroring her relief. He reached out to stroke the little girl's back, his touch so gentle it made her heart ache. Lucy went from her arms to his, as if needing Nate's strength. He held her close, his low voice and strong arms offering Lucy a solid male reassurance she didn't possess.

He'd be such a good father, if only he'd let himself believe in God's strength and endurance.

She summoned a shaky smile. "I knew you'd come for us."

His blue eyes were dark with concern. "I was almost too late."

She shook her head. "No, you were right on time."

He wrapped one arm around her shoulders, bringing her in for a three-way hug. "I put my faith in God and prayed. He showed me the way."

Her heart melted at his profession of faith. “I’m so glad to hear you say that.”

Nate pressed a kiss to her temple. “I couldn’t believe it when you turned to run toward me. Did you hear the stairs creaking?”

She shook her head, resting against him, breathing in his woodsy scent. She always felt safe and secure in Nate’s arms. But then she lifted her head to look up at him. “No, I didn’t hear the stairs creak at all, I just decided to run. Figured it was better than waiting to be—you know.” She didn’t want to use the words *shot and killed* in front of Lucy.

Murphy nudged Lucy’s foot, causing the little girl to shift in Nate’s arms to look down at him. “Good doggy,” she whispered.

“Yes, Murphy is a good doggy.” Willow was surprised at how silent the yellow Lab had been despite all the activity going on in the basement.

“You need to get home.” Nate’s voice held a note of remorse. “But I can’t go with you. I need to stay here.”

She felt herself tense. "Why? Because you fired in self-defense?"

He nodded. "Yes, and this means I'm on desk duty until the investigation is complete."

Desk duty? A frisson of fear streaked through her. "But I need you, Nate. What about the boss? Craggy Face told me his boss wanted to deal with me personally."

Nate's brow furrowed. "I heard them talking about some boss. I still don't understand why they want you, specifically."

"I don't know." She shivered and cast a worried glance over her shoulder. Even standing beside Nate in the alley, with cops surrounding them, didn't feel safe.

Was the guy in charge of this whole mess out there right now, watching them? Waiting for his chance to strike?

She instinctively moved closer to Nate, putting her hand over his where it rested on Lucy's back.

"It's obvious they're selling stolen goods," Nate continued. "There has to be hundreds of thousands of dollars' worth of merchandise down there. And clearly Damon Berk doesn't have the guts or the brains to be in charge of something this big."

"Please, Nate." She couldn't ignore the deep need to keep him close. "Don't leave us."

Nate hesitated, and glanced around. "Okay, listen, I don't want to leave you, Willow, but I have to stay at least for a while yet. Don't worry, I'll find someone to take you home and this time, I'll keep a K-9 team with you."

She tried to think of a way to change his mind. "What about the photograph?"

He glanced at her in confusion. "What about it? We already know Carl Dower was upset about you capturing his face."

"No, I think there's something more." She thought back to the way she'd edited the picture, blurring the background to bring the craggy features into sharper contrast. "I think I may have captured something else in the image."

"Like what?" There was an underlying urgency in his tone.

"I don't know. But Craggy Face made a comment that the boss was upset about the photograph being displayed at the community college. I didn't consider the photo being on display as a problem, but it doesn't matter because I think there's something else, too." She met his gaze. "I need to find the original digital file, see if I can bring the background into sharper focus. It may give us a clue as to who the big boss is."

Nate hesitated, and she could tell by the anguished expression on his face that his duty warred with the need to uncover the truth.

"Okay, we can check it out," he finally relented. "Shouldn't take too long to get the camera from the evidence room."

"Thanks, but I have all the originals on my computer at home, too." She released her breath in a soundless sigh of relief.

The photograph was the key; she just needed to figure out how to unlock the secrets buried within.

And maybe once they found the guy in charge, she and Lucy would be safe at last.

SEVENTEEN

Nate cuddled Lucy close, breathing in the calming scent of baby shampoo. He silently thanked God for giving him the strength he'd needed to save them.

The idea of losing Lucy or Willow was too much to bear.

He looked at his SUV parked at the end of the alley, knowing full well he shouldn't leave the scene of an officer-involved shooting. Yet he desperately wanted to take Willow and Lucy home. He told himself he was working the case, following a new lead, but he felt certain Sarge wouldn't see it that way.

Before he could so much as take a step toward his SUV, though, Vivienne and her border collie partner caught up to him. She scowled, glancing between him and Willow. "Slater, where are you going?"

"I need to take Willow and Lucy home." Even as he said the words, Vivienne's eyes widened and she quickly shook her head.

"You can't do that. You know the protocol." Vivienne glanced at Willow, who had taken Lucy from Nate's arms. Her expression softened. "I know you've been through a lot, Willow, and I know you're scared. But if you care about Nate at all, you won't let him risk his job for you."

"Now hold on," Nate began, but Vivienne cut him off.

"You can't leave. End of story."

"She's right." Willow's voice was low, soft and full of remorse. "I'm being selfish. You absolutely need to stay here and do your job, clear your name." Her smile looked wan. "We'll be okay. I'm sure one of the officers will escort us home."

He pushed down a surge of anger. No, they wouldn't be okay until they identified and arrested the big boss. The man who'd ordered Carl Dower to kidnap Willow and Lucy. The man in charge of this criminal endeavor, who ordered men, women and even a child to be killed without hesitation.

Leaving an officer on guard at her apartment hadn't prevented Willow from being taken against her will. From being threatened and almost killed.

No matter what happened to him, he couldn't bear the thought of failing to protect her again.

"I'll look at the original digital images and let you know what I find," Willow added.

"Digital images?" Vivienne raised a brow. "The ones you took of Carl Dower?"

"Yes." Willow looked tired but still wore the familiar stubborn expression on her face, the one that refused to quit, no matter what. "I want to examine it more closely."

Nate abruptly straightened. "I have an idea. My laptop is in my SUV, we'll pull up the photos on my computer and enlarge the image so we can see if there's anything in the background. We can also call Eden Chang for help. She's a genius when it comes to uncovering hidden secrets."

Vivienne didn't look entirely convinced

but nodded. "Fine, but don't leave the scene. Sarge is on his way and will want to talk to you."

"Understood." He put his hand beneath Willow's elbow. "Let's go. My SUV is at the end of the alley."

He led Willow through the mass of officers and crime scene techs to where he'd left his SUV only a short time ago, but it seemed like hours.

It was easy to remember the bitter taste of fear that had clogged his throat when he'd witnessed Dower dragging Willow into the back of the restaurant at gunpoint.

Thankfully, he'd gotten there in time. It had been the first time he'd ever shot a man in the course of duty, but looking back, he didn't see that he'd had an alternative.

Carl Dower had fired first, leaving him no choice but to take out the threat.

Still, he knew that while he had Willow as a witness, the evidence would have to be carefully examined in order to prove his side of the story.

Especially if Dower didn't survive his injury.

Shaking off the depressing thought, he opened the front driver's-side door, leaving it ajar to help air out the vehicle. Willow placed Lucy in the car seat from the other side of the SUV as he booted up the computer and then linked his phone to access the internet.

"We'll use the back. Murphy needs some water anyway." He carried the laptop around to the back of the SUV, opened the hatch and set the laptop down. Murphy gracefully leaped into the back, drank some water, then jumped back down.

"Let me access all my photos." Willow gestured to the screen. "Especially the one I took before I did the editing."

"Have at it." He watched over her shoulder as she logged in and pulled up the message and attached photo she'd sent to her photography instructor just ten days ago.

"This is the finished photo, after I blurred the background." Willow minimized the photograph and went back in her files. "The original one is here, somewhere."

"If you don't find it, I'll get an officer

to pick up your laptop and bring it here." Nate was anxious to see the original photograph on a large screen. There had to be something important that she'd unwittingly caught in the picture.

Something he should have thought about days ago, when she'd first shown him the photo on her digital camera. Had he let his emotional response to Willow and Lucy cloud his judgment?

As Willow worked, he stepped to the side and scanned the alley. Dower was hoisted into the back of an ambulance, the drivers no doubt rushing to take him to the closest hospital. Berk was still handcuffed and tucked in the back of a squad car. The crime scene techs were hard at work preserving evidence, but the number of cops that were around the area had dwindled.

The threat had been minimized and there were no doubt other calls coming in.

"I found it!" Willow's excited voice drew his attention back to her. "I think I see someone in the background but I can't make out the facial features."

"Send it to me, so I can forward the original to Eden."

"Okay." Seconds later, his phone pinged with a text message. He relayed it to Eden, then called her. "This is the original photograph that Willow took. Can you sharpen the background?"

"I'm putting together a digital timeline of Dower taking Willow and Lucy to the alley behind the restaurant. Sarge wants it ASAP."

"Okay, but this photo is important, too."

She sighed. "Okay, fine. I'll do my best and will call when I have something, okay?" Eden didn't wait for his response before disconnecting from the call.

"I'm getting it." Willow glanced up at him. "Eden probably has better skills, but it almost looks like a woman in the background."

"A woman?" He frowned, peering over her shoulder. The figure way in the back of the room did seem to have long blond hair. For a moment a flash of recognition flickered. "Deputy Mayor Theresa Gray."

"I knew you'd figure it out eventually." The scathing tone caused him to glance up in shocked surprise. The woman in the photograph was standing off to the side. In her hand she held a small yet lethal gun pointed directly at them. "Don't move, or I won't hesitate to shoot." She lifted the gun a little higher and pointed it first at Murphy, then back at Willow. "At this range, I won't miss."

Nate's heart thudded painfully in his chest. He'd found the true perpetrator a little too late.

"You're going to get into the SUV, slowly," Theresa Gray said. "Secure the dog in the back. Willow will slide in beside the brat, and you, Detective Slater, will get behind the wheel. We're going to take a little drive. Trust me, no one will stop a police car."

He glanced at Lucy, tucked into her car seat. She hadn't noticed the danger yet. He needed to find a way to neutralize the threat before Lucy had to suffer yet another traumatic event.

He faced the deputy mayor, hoping, praying someone would notice what was going on. But they were mostly hidden behind the SUV. And everyone assumed the danger was over.

If only he'd taken Willow and Lucy back to their apartment as he'd originally planned! Too late, now. He'd protect them both with his life, if he had to. He gathered his scattered thoughts together and cleared his throat, stalling for time. "This won't work. The original digital file has already been sent to our tech specialist. Killing us now will only make it worse. They'll easily figure out that you are the one behind all of this."

Instead of alarm, a slow, evil smile creased her features. "I've already thought of that. I always have a plan, unlike Dower, who's an incompetent idiot. It will be easy enough to pin this entire mess on Carl and Oscar Banjo."

His heart quickened. "How?"

"I'll claim I caught Dower in the restaurant talking to Berk as evidenced in the photo and suspected they were planning something. That I tried to figure out what it was, and soon realized Oscar Banjo was involved in something illegal."

"Selling stolen goods in the Basement Bargains store owned by Oscar Banjo," he said, finally putting the pieces together.

"Yes." Theresa's smile was smug. "My story will be that before I could go to the police, Dower kidnapped the woman." She waved a hand at the alley. "The rest happened because of Dower, and Banjo panicked. Once you're both gone and Banjo is arrested, there won't be anyone who can claim anything different. It will be my word against Oscar's, and, well, I'm the deputy mayor."

He didn't want to admit that she just might be able to pull it off.

"What about Berk?" Willow asked. "He knows the truth."

The deputy mayor lifted a thin shoulder. "Don't you know that accidents happen in jail all the time? Tsk, tsk." Her gaze hardened. "Now move!"

Nate lifted his hands in a gesture of surrender. The last thing he wanted to do was make the trigger-happy woman angry. Yet he knew there had to be a way out of this.

One that wouldn't cause any harm to come to Willow or Lucy.

Willow stepped around to the side of the vehicle. He took a step to follow her, glancing down at Murphy. They'd have to make their move soon.

Before it was too late.

Willow couldn't believe everyone around them was completely oblivious to what was going on. Granted there were fewer cops milling about, but several were standing and chatting nearby, unaware that they were being kidnapped by a crazy woman with a gun.

"Get in!" The terse order startled her.

"O-okay." Willow glanced at Nate and knew by the intensity of his gaze that he was going to risk his life to save them.

No! It couldn't end like this. She refused to let it end like this!

She abruptly leaped forward to the front

seat of the vehicle, slamming her fist onto the center of the steering wheel. The horn blared loudly, echoing off the brick buildings on either side of them.

In the same moment, Nate launched himself at the deputy mayor. "Get her, Murphy!"

The sharp retort of a gunshot could be heard above the sound of the horn. Finally, the officers who'd been standing just thirty feet away came running toward them.

"Nate! Nate!" He'd pinned Theresa Gray against the asphalt, his hands fighting for control of the weapon. Willow didn't see any blood, but feared the worst. "Someone please help him!"

After barking loudly in Theresa's face, Murphy shifted and grabbed her ankle in his teeth, clamping down tight enough to make her scream in outrage.

"Get him off me!"

That was all the advantage Nate needed. He yanked the gun from her grip and tossed it out of reach just as two officers joined the fray, surrounding them and helping Nate up and off Gray. In seconds they had the deputy mayor handcuffed.

Willow let out a ragged sigh of relief. This time, it was finally over.

Then she frowned. Bright crimson drops stained the white paint of the police SUV. What in the world? "Nate? Are you hurt?"

He stared at her blankly for a moment before glancing down at himself. Slowly, he put a hand up to the upper part of his left arm. The blue uniform was dark and when he pulled his palm away, it was covered in blood.

She gasped in horror. "She shot you!"

"Yeah." He looked surprised. "I hadn't noticed until now."

Tears pricked her eyes, but she quickly brushed them away. "We need an ambulance!" Feeling desperate, she turned to the front seat of the SUV. There had to be something she could use to help stop the bleeding.

"The glove box." Nate's voice was calm and sturdy despite the fact that he'd been shot. "And don't panic, it's just a flesh wound."

A flesh wound that was bleeding like a sieve. Opening the glove compartment, she found a first aid kit. Pulling out some gauze, she turned toward him and placed several white squares against the opening in the ripped sleeve of his shirt.

Seeing the wound up close, she realized he was right. The injury didn't look too serious, but was bad enough to need at least two layers of stitches. The amount of blood made her think an artery might have been hit.

"I knew you were going to jump toward her." She kept pressure against the pack of gauze. "I just knew it."

"Is that why you hit the horn?"

"Yes. I was hoping to get someone to pay attention."

The corner of his mouth quirked up in a lopsided grin. "Smart move. It startled her and caused her aim to go high and to the side. Probably saved my life."

Her eyes misted again. "I didn't know

what else to do. I absolutely didn't want to get into the car with her."

"Shh, it's okay." As if he wasn't injured, he pulled her close for a moment, brushing a kiss over her forehead. "It's over now for good."

She savored his embrace for a moment before pulling away, making room for the paramedics to move in. Feeling helpless to do anything more, she turned to Lucy, who had started to cry when the gun went off. Reaching into the back of the SUV, she gently pried her niece out of the car seat and into her arms.

"Shh, Lucy, it's okay. We're fine. Everything is going to be just fine."

Lucy gripped her tightly around the neck, buried her face in Willow's shoulder. It occurred to Willow that she'd said those same reassurances to Lucy several times now, but things hadn't been fine.

Just the opposite. They'd been in danger ever since the moment she'd brought Lucy home to live with her.

And as far as she knew, the police were

no closer to finding the mean clown with blue hair that had killed Lucy's parents. She knew the Brooklyn K-9 Unit was working hard on the case, though.

"I'm sorry, baby. I'm so sorry." She rested her cheek on Lucy's wavy hair. "You've been so brave."

"I wanna go home." Lucy's words were muffled against her neck.

Willow helplessly wondered if Lucy meant her apartment or her real home, the house she'd once shared with her parents.

"I know, baby. I know."

She hugged Lucy close, grateful the threat against them was over.

"I can walk." Ignoring Nate's protests, the paramedics assisted him onto the gurney. "It's not that bad."

"I think it's better to let the doctor decide that. You may need minor surgery to repair that wound." The paramedic near the head of the gurney rolled his eyes. "Why do our patients always think they know more than we do?"

"No clue," the paramedic at the foot responded.

"Hey, stop talking about me as if I'm not here." Nate scowled and winced as they tightened the straps around him. "It's just a flesh wound, and I'm not leaving without my partner. Murphy, come!"

The paramedics exchanged a long look. "Listen, buddy, your dog can't come with us."

"I can't leave him here." Nate levered himself upright. "I'll refuse to go with you. You can't force me."

"Nate, please." She reached out to lightly touch his uninjured arm. Her heart ached for him, and she realized how much she cared for this man she'd only known a short time. "Do as they say, okay? I'll take care of Murphy for you."

He shook his head. "I don't think Sarge will let you do that. Murphy is a cop. He'll have to go back to the precinct."

Vivienne stepped forward, her gaze full of concern. "I'll smooth things over with

Sarge. We can let Willow take Murphy for now. I can always pick him up later."

Willow wanted to weep with relief when Nate stopped fighting and nodded. "Okay, fine."

"We'll take good care of him." She forced a reassuring smile. "And we'll see you soon."

"No." The word came out so harsh she reared back as if he'd slapped her. "Listen, Willow, do me a favor and take Lucy and Murphy home, okay? You have both been through a lot, but you're safe now. There's no reason for you to come to the hospital. I'll be fine."

"Why not? I don't understand..." Her voice trailed off as the paramedic team began wheeling him toward the waiting rig.

She stared after them in shocked surprise. What was going on? Why didn't he want her to come to the hospital, to be there for him? Was this Nate's way of telling her their time together was over?

The thought of never seeing him again made her blood run cold. She'd hoped things would turn out differently once she and Lucy were safe. That maybe Nate would decide to give a relationship a try. Hadn't Nate admitted to putting his faith in God?

Then again, he'd made it clear he wasn't the kind of guy who wanted a family. Maybe he'd only used his father's anger and physical abuse as an excuse.

Maybe this was much more personal. That it was just Willow and Lucy he didn't want.

Nate and Murphy had saved their lives. It was more than anyone had ever done for her. She loved Nate, but would have to find a way to get over it. Time to stop wishing for things she couldn't have, to focus on the blessings God had granted.

She reached down to stroke Murphy's pale fur.

They were alive, and relatively unharmed, at least physically. Emotionally? Well, she knew Lucy would carry the psychological scars for a long time to come.

The best thing she could do for Nate was to support his decision. Despite the fact that every cell in her body wanted to scream in protest, she told herself to move on.

Nate had sacrificed himself for them.

The least she could do was let him go without a fuss.

EIGHTEEN

Considering he hadn't realized that he'd been shot, it was amazing that now that he was aware of the injury, his left arm throbbed worse than a sore tooth. Nate hated being in the ambulance and in the Emergency Department; playing the role of helpless victim wasn't his thing. He was relieved when the doctor had announced that once the wound was cleaned and stitched and he'd been given antibiotics, as bullets were obviously considered to be a source of infection, he was free to go.

As he waited for the antibiotic to drip through his IV, he tried to forget the wounded expression in Willow's eyes when he'd told her not to come see him. He closed his eyes against the harsh overhead lights, telling himself he'd done the right thing. Better to have a clean break.

The danger was over. She didn't need him anymore.

But the idea of not seeing her and Lucy again hurt at a visceral level, far worse than the physical discomfort in his upper arm.

The events outside the SUV replayed over and over in his head like a stuck video loop. The moment of searing anger that had hit him seconds before he'd launched himself at the deputy mayor at the exact same time Willow had hit the horn.

Taking her down to the asphalt and fighting for the gun.

He'd managed to hold his anger in check as the officers had pulled him off the woman who'd tried to kill him and Willow, but he'd been secretly horrified at his reaction.

The idea that he might be more like his father than he realized wouldn't leave him alone.

And it had forced him to realize Willow and Lucy were better off without him. He may have fallen for Willow and the adorable Lucy, but they would be fine. Better, probably, without him.

"Detective Slater?" He opened his eyes when a nurse lightly touched his arm. "There's someone here to see you."

Willow? His heart soared with anticipation, but when he turned to look at the person standing in the doorway, a K-9 at her side, disappointment stabbed deep. Still, he forced a smile. "Vivienne, what are you doing here?"

"Checking in." Her brow furrowed with concern. "Sarge wants an update on your condition."

"I'm fine." He didn't want or need sympathy from his team. Bad enough that he hadn't figured out what was going on until it was too late.

Until he'd almost lost the woman and little girl he cared about more than anything.

More than himself.

"Hmm." She stared at the IV. "Are you sure about that?"

"Yeah." He shifted on the gurney. "They're letting me out of here as soon as the meds are in. It's just a flesh wound, only needed about a dozen stitches. Nothing bad enough to keep me off duty for very long."

"It sure bled enough." Vivienne stepped closer, her expression full of concern. "I'm sorry I stopped you from taking Willow and Lucy home. If I had let you go..." Her voice trailed off.

"Not your fault. You were right about sticking to protocol." Granted, the same thought had filtered through his mind, but it was ridiculous to play the what-if game. For all he knew, the deputy mayor might have followed them to Willow's, where the outcome could have been much worse. "Besides, I have a feeling she was hanging around there for a while, waiting for us. Leaving earlier likely wouldn't have changed anything."

"Maybe not," Vivienne conceded. "Listen, I have to head back to the station. Gavin called another staff meeting, wants us there in an hour."

He glanced up at the IV that was still dripping. "The antibiotic is almost finished. Do you mind giving me a ride? I'd like to be there."

"Sure, why not? Your SUV is being processed as part of the crime scene, anyway."

"Great." He couldn't deny being anxious to get out of here. "All this fuss over a flesh wound."

"I'm pretty sure that even a flesh wound can get infected." Vivienne tipped her head to the side, her expression turning thoughtful. "Why did you tell Willow not to visit?"

He glanced away, unable to maintain eye contact. "I won't be here long enough to warrant a visit. Besides, it's better for her and Lucy."

"Yeah, but why? It's obvious she cares about you, and I'm fairly certain the feeling is mutual."

No way was he revealing the truth about his father's abuse. Willow was the only one he'd told, and he planned to keep it that way.

"Never mind, I shouldn't have asked." She glanced up at the IV. "I'm going to call Sarge, tell him we'll be there shortly."

As she stepped away to use her phone, he

realized Vivienne didn't have Murphy with her, which meant he'd have to pick up his partner himself. Despite the fact that he had tried to make a clean break with Willow, for her sake and Lucy's, it appeared he'd be seeing her again soon.

Probably for the last time.

It was pathetic how grateful he was to have one more chance to see her prior to saying goodbye. Before he walked away, leaving his heart behind.

When he and Vivienne arrived at the station, the rest of the team was already gathered around the large oval table.

Gavin raised a brow when he saw Nate. "You sure you're okay?"

"Doc said I'm fine, just a minor lifting restriction for a couple of days." He took a seat between Max Santelli, one of the newer members of the Brooklyn K-9 Unit, and his buddy, Officer Ray Morrow.

"You're on modified until the investigation into the shooting of Carl Dower has been completed anyway, so it's no problem."

Gavin swept his gaze over the rest of the team. "There are a few things I wanted to let you all know about. You may have noticed that the media has caught wind of the Emery murders having a similar MO to the McGregor case."

K-9 detective Bradley McGregor scowled. Nate knew how hard all this had to be on him—his parents killed twenty years ago. The killer suddenly back, committing a very similar double homicide. Nate froze. Was it the same killer? Or could it be a copycat?

"Noticed? Penny and I have been dodging reporters for the past twenty-four hours."

"Sorry about that." Gavin spread his hands. "At least this time, they seem to have focused on the fact that you were working during the time frame of the murders, so you're not a suspect."

"Yeah, sure." Bradley looked glum. "I never should have been a suspect in the first place."

"I know." Gavin smiled reassuringly. "I also want to congratulate Ray Morrow and his K-9 partner, Abby, for stopping a drug runner who was delivering two large suitcases of prescription opioids through the subway."

Ray shifted, looking uncomfortable with the praise. "Thanks, but Abby's nose gets the credit."

"Nice job." Nate grinned. "Did you get the guy in charge?"

"Not yet." Ray shrugged. "Idiot is refusing to talk, other than making stupid threats."

Gavin's gaze narrowed. "What kind of threats?"

"You know, things like, 'Watch your back' and 'The boss is gonna get you for this.' The usual garbage."

"Two suitcases full of dope is a lot," Gavin pointed out. "You need to take those threats seriously. Back off the case for a while, until things cool off."

"Sure," Ray agreed, but as soon as Gavin changed topics, he leaned toward Nate. "I'm not backing off," he whispered. "I won't stop pulling deliverymen off the streets until I catch the kingpin in charge of bringing drugs through Brooklyn."

"Just be careful, okay?" Nate knew that once Ray put his mind to something, there was no changing it. "Keep your head down."

"I will." Ray straightened, a fierce determination in his eyes.

"Okay, that's it for now." Gavin slowly rose to his feet. "You're all dismissed. Oh, and Nate?"

He paused, turned back to his boss. "Yeah?"

"Where's Murphy?"

"I'm picking him up right now." Nate gave Gavin a nod and headed out of the precinct.

As he made his way to Willow's apartment, he hoped and prayed he'd have the strength of will to ignore his desire to continue seeing her on a personal level. To hold back from telling her how much he'd come to care about her and Lucy.

For her sake and his own sanity. No sense in longing for something he couldn't have.

A family.

Her apartment seemed incredibly lonely without Nate's presence. Murphy helped, but she knew the K-9's visit was temporary.

After she'd cleaned up Officer Kuhn's blood from the floor, spoke to Jayne Hendricks about a child psychologist for Lucy and made an early dinner for her niece, she stared blindly out the window at the city streets below, wondering how Nate was doing.

In hindsight, she shouldn't have been surprised by Nate's refusal to have her come visit. Hadn't she tried to mentally prepare herself for this? She knew from personal experience that men didn't stick around.

They didn't want the same things she did, like a home, a family.

Maybe his concern over turning out like his father was nothing more than an excuse to avoid becoming emotionally involved. After all, her father had been nonexistent, disappearing when she was two years old, Alex only four. Then after their mother died, they'd been raised by their grandparents.

Maybe Nate was right, that it was better to avoid becoming entangled in something that you knew you couldn't handle long term.

Yet as soon as the theory formed in her

mind, she rejected it. Nate had held her in his arms, had kissed her, twice. He'd held and kissed Lucy, too, caring for her the way a father would.

It was irritating how Nate was selling himself short; he had a great capacity for love and caring.

But maybe not with her and Lucy.

Well. Enough with the pity party already. She'd just have to remember she'd played a role in helping Nate find his way to faith and God. Wasn't that more important?

A knock at the door startled her. Murphy scrambled to his feet, going on alert. For a moment a frisson of fear snaked down her spine, but she told herself the danger was over. Besides, she felt certain Murphy would alert her to danger, but he was staring at the door, his tail wagging with anticipation.

Still, she checked the peephole to see who was out there.

Nate?

Her pulse spiked, then beat so erratically she had to take a moment to calm herself before opening the door. "Hi. Have you been released from the hospital already?"

"Yep." Murphy rushed over to greet Nate as if the K-9 hadn't seen him in days instead of a couple of hours. She couldn't help smiling at how the two of them looked together. After giving Murphy a good rub, Nate rose to his feet. "Told you it was just a flesh wound. I never should have gotten in the stupid ambulance."

"I'm just glad you're okay." She wanted to throw herself into his arms but forced herself to stay back. "I suppose you're here for Murphy?"

"Yes, I need to take him home."

"I'm sure Murphy missed you." *I missed you.*

"No! I don't want Murphy to go!" Lucy's plaintive tone made her wince. The little girl threw her arms around Murphy's neck, burying her face against his fur. "I want him to stay!"

"I know, baby, but Murphy and Nate work together as a team. They're both police officers." She gently extricated the animal from Lucy's grip and pulled her up and into her arms.

Nate put Murphy on his leash. "Well, I guess this is it."

She didn't want to agree with him, but she wouldn't force him to stay, either. "I guess so. Take care of yourself."

"I will." Nate stared at her for a long moment, as if there was so much more he wanted to say. Or maybe it was just that her heart wanted him to say something more.

"Bye, Willow, Lucy." His smile didn't quite reach his eyes as he opened the door.

"Nate, please don't go." The words escaped before she could stop them.

He stood for a long moment, then glanced at her over his shoulder. The stark longing on his face ripped at her heart. "I have to."

"No, you don't." She set Lucy on her feet and moved toward him. She couldn't just let him walk away without even trying to reach him. "I—have something to tell you."

"Willow, you don't have to…"

"I love you." She practically flung the words at him. "I love you, Nate Slater! You can go ahead and walk out that door, but it won't stop me from loving you."

This time, his mouth gaped comically, as if she'd said something he didn't understand. "What? No, you don't."

"Yes, I do." She took another step toward him. "I understand you don't feel the same way about me, but I wanted, needed you to know the truth."

"But—" He shook his head. "It can't work, Willow. You don't know the real me, the person deep inside."

His words offered a glimmer of hope. "I do know the person you are deep inside. You're kind, loyal, brave, smart and so much more."

"Angry." He said the word with a bitterness that made her wince. "You forgot about angry."

She threw up her hands in exasperation. "What are you talking about? Everyone gets mad, and sad, and frustrated and annoyed—none of that means you're a bad person."

A flicker of uncertainty passed over his face. "But my father…"

"Was a mean and abusive man." She took another step, close enough now that she could place her hand on his uninjured shoulder. "Did you know that most abuse is more about power and control than anger? Sure, sometimes people get mad enough to lash out, but you've never done that, have you?"

A look of anguish filled his eyes. "I want to say no, but I was furious at the deputy mayor when I tackled her to the pavement."

Really? That's what this was about? "Nate, your action saved our lives. Not because you were mad at her, but to get the gun away from her." Now she found herself growing irritated. "You can't possibly equate that action to what your father did to you and your mother."

"Maybe not, but the flash of anger I felt inside..." He shrugged. "I was afraid there was more of my father in me than I realized."

"Nate, you're not your father. And you'll never be your father." She pressed her hand firmly against him, turning him so that he faced her. "And you know why? Because

God will never let you be that man. God will guide you, and protect you, and cherish you. As long as you believe in Him, you'll never fall into the depths your father sank to."

He reached up and covered her hand with his, searching her gaze. "You really believe that?"

"Absolutely."

"Willow." He slowly but firmly drew her into his arms. "I want more than anything to kiss you."

That made her smile. "I'm not stopping you."

His warm embrace and possessive kiss filled her with hope and anticipation. But the kiss didn't last long, as Lucy came over to tug on the hem of her hoodie.

"Aunt Willow, I wanna hug, too."

Nate lifted his head and chuckled. He readily bent down and picked Lucy up, then pulled Willow in close. "Okay, now we're all hugging together."

Tears blurred her vision at how easily he accepted Lucy into their embrace. This was exactly how she imagined her life to be.

His gaze met hers over Lucy's head. "I love you, too, Willow. I don't know why it's taken me so long to realize the importance of focusing on the good things in my life, like you and Lucy."

Her breath caught in her throat. "Are you sure?"

"Yes. I'm sure." He kissed her again, then kissed Lucy's cheek. "I love both of you."

"I love you," Lucy said. "And Murphy, too."

That made her laugh. "I guess it's unanimous."

"Yes." Nate's gaze lingered on hers. "I promise that I won't stop searching for the man responsible for stealing the lives of your brother and his wife."

"I know." While a part of her worried about Nate's safety, she understood that this was part of being in a relationship with a cop.

And she'd gladly take him as is.

"Are we a family?"

Lucy's innocent question caught her off guard. She glanced at Nate, unsure how to answer. But then Lucy pointed at the dog. "I wanna hug Murphy." Lucy wiggled in

Nate's arms until he set her on her feet. She ran over to the yellow Lab and wrapped her arms around his neck.

The two of them were adorable together.

Nate cleared his throat. "I know you're just getting used to having Lucy around, but I need to ask you something."

Her heart raced. "Ask me what?"

He stared deep into her eyes. "Willow, will you do me the honor of becoming my wife?"

She blinked, fearing she'd misunderstood. Hearing he loved her was one thing, but she hadn't expected this. "You…want to get married?"

"Yes, I want to marry you." Love shimmered in his gaze, and as he tugged her close, he glanced down at Lucy and Murphy. "I'd like to make you and Lucy a part of my family. Lucy deserves a father, a family. If you'll have me."

"Oh, Nate. That's exactly what I want, too." She rested her head on Nate's shoulder. "You'll be a great father and husband. I hope I can be just as good of a mother and wife."

"I love you, Willow. And we'll do this together, with God's blessing." He kissed her again and Willow knew that she'd cherish this moment, forever.

* * * * *

Look for Raymond Morrow's story,
Chasing Secrets *by Heather Woodhaven,*
the next book in the
True Blue K-9 Unit: Brooklyn series,
available in May 2020.

TRUE BLUE K-9 UNIT: BROOKLYN

These police officers fight for justice with
the help of their brave canine partners.

Copycat Killer *by Laura Scott,*
April 2020

Chasing Secrets *by Heather Woodhaven,*
May 2020

Deadly Connection *by Lenora Worth,*
June 2020

Explosive Situation *by Terri Reed,*
July 2020

Tracking a Kidnapper *by Valerie Hansen,*
August 2020

Scene of the Crime *by Sharon Dunn,*
September 2020

Cold Case Pursuit *by Dana Mentink,*
October 2020

Delayed Justice *by Shirlee McCoy,*
November 2020

True Blue K-9 Unit Christmas: Brooklyn
by Laura Scott and Maggie K. Black,
December 2020

Dear Reader,

It's such an honor to be included in this amazing group of authors to write these wonderful K-9 stories. This year I'm blessed to kick off the True Blue K-9 Unit: Brooklyn series. I hope you enjoy reading about the new Brooklyn K-9 Unit and the team that is working hard to keep the streets of New York safe.

I hope you enjoy the upcoming books in the series; they are incredible stories. And of course, you'll want to find out who killed the Emerys and the McGregors.

I always enjoy hearing from my readers. You can find me through my website at https://www.laurascottbooks.com, on Facebook at https://www.facebook.com/LauraScottBooks and on Twitter at https://twitter.com/laurascottbooks. I offer an exclusive and free novella to all newsletter subscribers, so sign up now through my website to get your copy.

Yours in faith,
Laura Scott